His Sitting Tenant

By

Linda Jones

Other books by Linda Jones

The Angel
ISBN:978-1-4259-9772-9
Witch Hunt
BN:978-1-4628-9650-9
The Lost Heiress
ISBN:978-1-3264-5735-8

The Mysterious Miss Hawthorne
ISBN:978-1-3264-4939-1
Tenuous Connections
ISBN:978-0-244-95360-7

Heartsong
ISBN:978-0-244-71718-6

Children of Eden
ISBN:978-0-244-80410-7

Claiming Samantha
ISBN-13:9798581385104

Once and or Always
ISBN-978-1-916820-42-5
Dear Max
ISBN-978-1-916981-80-5

Prologue

Australia 1872

Noah read through the letters several times before taking them to his grandfather. Ernest Laing was in his nineties but his mind was as clear as ever. As he had spent some time in England, Noah hoped he could throw some light on this strange correspondence.

Noah paused at the doorway to the veranda and looked at the old man, apparently asleep, in a wide cane chair. He had been Noah's guardian, mentor and friend for more than twenty years. They had shared adventures, travelling around the vast country, seldom staying anywhere for long. Now they were settled and dozing in his chair and reliving his memories.

'Gramp,' Noah called quietly.

Ernest opened his eyes and said, gruffly, 'I wasn't asleep. Just thinking.'

Noah handed him the letters. 'Tell me what you think about this.' Ernest put on his spectacles and started to read. Noah leant against the veranda post and watched the expressions on the wrinkled face. Frowning concentration was replaced by sadness. Ernest closed his eyes and gave a shuddering sigh. The papers fell from his hands and fluttered to the floor.

'Gramp? Do you know what this is about?'

Ernest looked up with tears in his eyes and shook his head wearily. 'I'm sorry, lad. You will have to go.'

'I am not leaving you!' Noah declared. His grandfather's health was failing. Common sense said he did not have much longer to live.

Ernest shook his head again. 'Now they have found us, they won't give up.'

Noah didn't understand and simply asked, 'Who is George Laing?'

'My brother.'

Chapter 1

Noah breathed a sigh of relief when his boots hit the solid stone of the English dock. Wearing a wide-brimmed hat and crumpled clothes that hung loosely on his tall frame, he looked like a scarecrow. Despite his name, Noah had proved to be a very poor sailor. The long journey from Australia had been a series of nightmares, culminating in a ferocious storm in the Bay of Biscay, when he had prayed to die.

He would surely have done so if not for the tender care of Bill Norton, a gentle giant who had nursed him as tenderly as any mother. He had cleaned up the vomit and trickled fluids into Noah's reluctant stomach.

Bill's bland expression and slow speech made him appear half-witted, but it was a façade he had erected to stay out of trouble. He had discovered early on that instant obedience and keeping his mouth shut was the best way to survive the harsh life of a transported convict. Behind the mask was a sharp mind and a dogged determination to return to England. Without money or influence, he had been working for his passage and had cannily adopted the wealthy but suffering passenger in the hope of future reward.

That was how it had started, but the two men, so different in class, stature and health, had formed a mutual respect and friendship.

Bill nudged Noah forward and asked, 'What do we do now, mate? You shouldn't be standing around in this cold wind.'

'We get as far from this blasted ocean as fast as we can,' Noah replied wryly. 'If I never see more than enough water to fill a bathtub I will be satisfied.'

Porters and touts rushed forward, offering transport and accommodation. Noah chose a ragged youth who led them to a line of carts and carriages. Bill heaved their bags into the bag of a fairly clean carriage, helped Noah into the interior and climbed up beside the driver. Noah tossed a coin to the boy and sat back to contemplate his future.

He had received the summons to come to England over a year ago. The letter had been forwarded by Mr Wesley Harris, of Harris, Son and Browning, legal advisers to Baron Laing, of Laington Manor, Stapleton, Gloucestershire, England. Apparently, Noah was the baron's heir. The present baron was the brother of Noah's grandfather and wanted Noah to come and 'learn to be a gentleman!' Not the most tactful invitation, but understandable as little was generally known about conditions in Australia.

What little Noah knew of conditions in England was blurred by the conflicting views of his father and grandfather. Gramp said it was ruled by hidebound snobs who thought more of possessions than people. Noah's father had seen it as a well-ordered society far removed from the felon-infested land into which he had been born. Noah had not had much to do with the convicts, but the increasing number of free settlers who had come in search of a better life tended to endorse Gramp's opinion.

So far Noah had found England cold, wet and overcrowded.

The carriage jerked to a halt, shaking Noah from his thoughts. The future could wait. Now he wanted a bed that did not sway and a chance to regain his strength before visiting the lawyer who had contacted him.

Three days later, Noah was in London. He had spent the intervening days recovering from the journey. He cut a very different figure from his arrival. Food that stayed in his stomach, a haircut and new clothing had transformed him into a very personable gentleman.

He had been horrified when he looked in the hotel mirror. He was most likely to be tossed into the street if he turned up at the lawyer's office looking like a tramp. Bill looked even worse and stank of the animals had tended on the voyage. He had been refused admittance to the first hotel they'd tried and been directed to a public bathhouse.

Noah had needed to present his credentials to a bank before they could buy new clothes. He did not know the extent of his inheritance or how long it would take to dispose of it, but he was already wealthy. A letter from his Australian bank would ensure he had available funds for the immediate future.

Another immediate task was to send a letter to his mother, telling her of his safe arrival. With any luck he would be on his way home before she received it.

Noah visited the lawyer looking a very different figure than he had cut on arrival in England. Food that stayed in his stomach, a haircut and new clothing had transformed him into a very personable gentleman.

He had sent a message to Mr Harris, the lawyer, who had contacted him, and was expected. He was admitted by a servant and at the mention of his name, he had no need to state the purpose of his visit and was shown into a waiting room smelling of dust and furniture polish. He did not have long to wait before he was escorted to a large office on the first floor.

The man who came forward to meet him was younger than Noah had expected. The Mr Harris who had forwarded Baron Laing's letter had claimed long acquaintance with the old man.

Noah's puzzlement was cleared when the young man said, 'I am Richard Harris. Welcome to England, Lord Laing. Please take a seat.' When Noah was settled and about to comment, the solicitor continued. 'I have recently taken over from my father, who is in poor health, but I have all the documents here.' He tapped a brown bundle on his desk. 'I expect you are eager to know the details?'

Noah shook his head. He felt no excitement about what he would be told as he intended to dispose of the property as soon and possible and return to Australia. He had only come at Gramp's insistence and had delayed his departure until Ernest died. Things Gramp had told him after he received the letter had piqued his curiosity and he needed to re-evaluate his life. The past could never be recaptured but still held enough promise to lure him back home.

He did need to query one thing. 'You called me Lord Laing. Am I to assume the baron has died?'

'Sadly, yes. I never met him but my father said he was, um…'
Harris pursed his lips, considering his words. 'Shall we say
somewhat eccentric?'

'In what way?'

Harris fidgeted with the folder. 'Perhaps I should go through
his will, step by step.'

Noah lounged in his seat and listened politely through the
legal rigmarole and generous bequests. Mr Harris took a deep
breath. 'To my daughter-in-law, Lois Laing, I leave a lifetime
tenancy of Laington Manor and an allowance of £500 per annum.
I also appoint said Lois Laing as trustee of the Laington estate
until such time as she deems Noah Laing fit to assume control.'

Noah jerked upright and let out an exclamation of surprise and
annoyance. 'What?' he demanded. Until now he'd had little
interest in the matter, but it was insulting to be deemed incapable
of managing an estate and beholden to a woman!

Mr Harris looked very uncomfortable. 'I am sorry. It is most
unusual and I would have strongly advised against it. I
understand Mrs Laing was tutored by the baron and has, for the
past several years, virtually run the estate. My father admired Mrs
Laing and said she was very capable.' The solicitor's doubtful
expression said he did not agree.

'Now she has full control over my head! What nonsense! This
cannot be legal.'

'I am afraid Lord Laing foresaw your objections. If you will
allow me to continue.'

Noah sat in growing disbelief us he heard that in the event of
any attempt to break the will, the whole of Lord Laing's personal
fortune would revert to the crown. Mr Harris stopped speaking
and handed Noah the document. Noah read the words, 'And let
anyone try to get it back!' Noah laughed. No wonder the solicitor
was reluctant to read that out.

'Well,' he said with a puff of annoyance. 'I have wasted my
time. If I was not reluctant to face another sickness-ridden
journey so soon I would be on the next boat back to Australia!'

'Please don't be hasty, my lord. The contents of the house
alone are worth a fortune.'

'I don't need a fortune. I need to know how I can get rid of Mrs Laing and dispose of the estate.'

Mr Harris sat forward in alarm. 'Dispose of it? The title and a small amount of land are entailed. I have never heard of anyone renouncing a title. They will probably revert to the crown but I hope it will not come to that.' He ran his hand gently over the inventory. 'I am sure you will change your mind once you have seen what is involved. We will find a way of coming to some arrangement with Mrs Laing.'

Reluctantly, Noah listened to the solicitor's arguments. He was still seething with resentment, but his natural sense of humour was beginning to kick in. Why was he so incensed when he did not want the estate anyway? It was a farce. Perhaps it would be diverting to meet Mrs Laing. It would at least take his mind off his recent sorrows, and he really did want to see something of England while he was here.

Noah returned to his hotel pondering the recent revelations. The situation at Laington had all the elements of a theatrical comedy. The inhabitants were clearly expecting a rough, uneducated colonial who needed to be taught his manners. The more he told Bill about his interview the funnier it seemed.

'Don't they have a hencoop for the old females?' Bill asked.

'A dower house, you mean? Yes and no. The dower house, call Laington Grace, is a separate property owned outright by the female line. The last baroness had no female relatives and left it to her maid.' Noah sniggered. 'Mr Harris hinted that she may have been the old baron's mistress!'

Bill scratched his head. 'A rum do all round.' He looked away for a moment. 'I expect you want to be on your way to sort it out.'

'Not before we sort out your problems.' Noah smiled. 'I promised to help you find your family and I do not forget that you literally saved my life.'

Bill shrugged. It was a typical reaction. He had received little praise or appreciation in his life and did not know how to deal with thanks.

'Get on with you. You needed help and I had little else to do.' Which was not quite true. Bill had been employed to work with the livestock, which had been the boat's main cargo.

'I don't know where to start,' Bill admitted with a sigh. 'The old house we lived in was due to be pulled down. Ma and the kids had nowhere else to go.' This was old news to Noah, but he refused to believe it was a hopeless quest. Money had a way of revealing information where mere questions failed.

'Bear up, my friend. I can't promise to find your family but we can discover what happened to them.' Good or bad, Noah thought silently. Eighteen years was a long time, particularly for those in need. Losing loved ones was hard, but worrying about the living must be even worse.

Chapter 2

Lois sang softly as she drove her pony trap along the lane. After a week of constant rain, the wind had dropped and the sun was visible through a thin layer of cloud. She had taken the opportunity to inspect the western portion of the estate as the Mill Field was prone to flooding. Fortunately the river had not breached its banks. Her optimistic mood heightened when she spotted a few early primroses in the verge. Spring was on its way.

It had been a dreary few weeks since Mr Harris had written to tell her the new baron had arrived in England. As expected, he was not pleased with the conditions imposed by George's will. She was not entirely happy with them herself, but Laington was too precious to be handed to an incompetent. If Noah Laing was anything like his grandfather, he would squander his inheritance in short order.

Lois was not sure how she would deal with a resentful man. Mr Harris had given no clue as to the new baron's character but, given the delay in his arrival, Lois wondered if he had spent his time exploring the London fleshpots. It did not bode well for the future.

The sound of an approaching horse penetrated the thick hedge that separated the lane from the main drive. Had his tardy lordship arrived at last? Well, she was not going to change her plans for the day to hurry back to greet him. She was going to take tea with Hattie! 'So there!' she muttered with a naughty smile.

Noah's first view of Laington Manor was lightened by a sudden burst of sunlight. It warmed the grey stone edifice and sparkled on its many windows. It stood at the end of a wide avenue and was framed like a picture by a high stone wall. The central part of the building was a square protrusion, slightly higher than the wings and topped by a flagpole. A porch covered the wide door and, as he drew closer, he could see that the drive went through the structure, allowing passengers to alight from their carriages under cover.

A young lad ran from the right side of the building and looked at him with interest. 'Are you the new baron?' he asked.

'Yes. I am here to see Mrs Laing.'

'She's not here.'

'That will be enough, Thomas!' called the elderly man who had emerged from the front door. He turned to Noah and bent his head. Not a bow, just an acknowledgement of his gentlemanly bearing. 'Lord Laing?' he enquired and, at Noah's nod, said, 'Welcome to Laington, my Lord. I am Pound, the butler. Thomas will take your horse while I show you inside.'

Noah glanced at the lad. 'He said Mrs Laing is not here.'

'Not at present but I am sure she will return shortly. Thomas will see to your horse. Please come inside.'

For some reason Noah was reluctant to enter the house. Under the present conditions he was subordinate to Mrs Laing, and it seemed rude to take possession of the house in her absence. 'Do you know where she might be?'

Pound considered for a moment. 'She has been inspecting the estate but is most likely to call on Miss Brown on her way back.'

'At Laington Grace?' he commented wryly.

'Just so, my lord.'

'I will ride in that direction. I assume it is the house down there.'

Noah waved his hand towards a lane that joined the main drive. He had spotted a roof over the hedge and did not expect there to be any other houses in the vicinity. Pound nodded again and Noah prepared to leave, but not before he noticed the butler gesture to the boy who shot away, giving him a head start. Presumably to warn his mistress.

Noah made no effort to overtake him and followed slowly. It amused him to think that Mrs Laing would be flustered at not being available to greet him. The fact that she would visit a woman of low repute who had effectively ousted her from a rightful claim to Laington Grace intrigued him. The next few days promised to be interesting.

'I think the new baron may have arrived,' Lois said as she entered Hattie's sitting room.

'And hard on your heels. Young Thomas came dashing in a few minutes ago.' Hattie cocked her head and grinned. 'That sounds like him now.'

Noah saw a pony and empty trap tied to the fence and hesitated. 'Damn.' He did not want to follow her into a stranger's house uninvited. Meeting her out in the open would have put them on an even footing. He turned back the way he had come, determined to while away the time exploring more of his inheritance.

'He's leaving,' Hattie said from her position at the window. She let the curtain fall and resumed her seat by the fire. She was middle-aged and dressed entirely in black. She had a pleasant, pale face topped by a coronet of plaited dark hair. It gave her a slightly regal look.

By contrast, her visitor was warmly dressed in a tweed coat and rosy-cheeked from her cold drive. Lois started to pull on the leather gloves she had just removed and sighed. 'I suppose I had better go and meet him.'

'No,' Hattie insisted. 'Don't go chasing after him. He has kept you waiting long enough.'

Lois agreed. But he was the baron and entitled to a courteous welcome. Even so, she took her time over her goodbye, ending with a request that Hattie joined them for dinner.

From his position on a slight rise, Noah saw the trap return. He was partially hidden by a stand of trees and took the opportunity to take in her appearance. She was wearing a knitted cap that covered her hair while exposing her beautiful face. She was younger than he expected given that she was the widow of the elderly baron's son. Too young to be running an extensive property. For a moment he wondered if this was indeed Mrs Laing. From his time in London he had learned that ladies did not commonly drive themselves around unaccompanied. On the other hand, who else would be visiting Miss Brown?

The young lad ran to meet her, talking excitedly. Noah was too far away to hear the words but guessed she was being given a potted version of his arrival. He gave her time to enter the house before resuming his ride. She would not be best pleased to be caught in her dishevelled state and he did not want to start off on the wrong foot.

Lois was pacing the floor when Noah Laing was finally announced. The wretched man had a habit of keeping her waiting. She had changed into a respectable winter dress of fine, pink wool which complemented her fair complexion. Her hair was plainly drawn back into a knot at her neck, but she twiddled with a loose strand that had escaped, trying to tuck it back behind her ear. She tensed at sounds of an arrival in the hall and took a deep breath to calm her nerves.

'Lord Laing,' Pound announced from the doorway. He stood aside for Noah to enter the room.

Lois's heart gave a little skip. He was a fine specimen of manhood with wide shoulders and the taut leg muscles of a rider. Medium brown hair with lighter streaks was clipped short but showed a tendency to curl over his ears. His clean-shaven face revealed the classic Laing wide brow and square chin, and his skin was more tanned than one who had spent the winter in England. Piercing blue eyes gazed back at her before he bowed. 'Mrs Laing.'

Devoid of her thick coat and hat, Noah could see that Mrs Laing was small, with a dainty figure and fair hair softly drawn back to reveal a heart-shaped face. She stood still as a statue, only her eyes moving to flick over him before she replied, 'My Lord,' and bobbed a shallow curtsey.

Pound was hovering in the doorway and Lois ordered tea. 'Or would you prefer something stronger?' she queried.

'A bit early in the day,' Noah replied. 'But coffee would be preferable if it is available.'

Pound left, closing the door behind him.

'Won't you be seated.'

'I am pleased to meet you.'

Both spoke at the same time and gave a small laugh. It broke the ice and they sat facing each other on either side of a wide fireplace.

'Did you have a pleasant journey?' Lois asked politely.

'No, it was horrendous. Long weeks of storms and seasickness. England greeted me with a howling gale and temperatures low enough to freeze the blood.'

It was a frank statement, spoken without self-pity.

'I expect you are used to hot weather all the time.'

'We do get cold weather but I left in mid-summer when the temperature can rise to over one hundred degrees.'

It was a banal conversation and Lois was relieved when a maid arrived with the tea tray. She arranged the set at Lois's elbow, turning the handles of the tea and coffee pots for easy reach. Lois busied herself with pouring the drinks and racking her brains for another topic of conversation. Noah raised his eyes to the high, elaborately plastered ceiling and was equally at a loss as to how to continue. The maid passed him his drink and left the room.

Lois met his eyes over the rims of their cups. He really was quite handsome. But that was beside the point. Lowering her teacup, she said, 'The master suite has been prepared for you. One of the footmen will attend you until you employ a valet.'

'I don't need a valet. I have been dressing myself since I was three years old.'

'But that was in—'

'A barbaric land far from civilisation,' Noah said, completing the sentence. 'We are not all savages, Mrs Laing. We have cities and polite society when needed. I attended university but prefer the freedom of my sheep station.'

'You know about sheep.' Lois sighed with relief. 'We have a large flock at Laington. It will give you a starting point.'

Noah doubted her flock was anywhere near the size of the one he had left behind. To start with, England did not have room for stations that stretched for miles in all directions, but this was not the time to brag.

Sheep were a safe topic, followed by general agriculture. It carried them through the rest of their refreshments. Eventually, Lois rang for the tray to be removed and suggested that Noah might like to go to his room.

It was a dismissal of sorts, but Noah declined the invitation. 'I am staying in a hotel in town with my companion. I will leave now and return tomorrow.' It was a decisive statement and Lois was secretly relieved. Perhaps, by tomorrow, she would have regained her wits enough to embark on a sensible regime for acquainting his lordship with the extent and responsibilities of his inheritance.

Noah's hired horse was brought to the door by a small, bow-legged man who Lois introduced as Farmer, the stable master. As he handed over the reins, Farmer commented, 'We have better mounts than this poor nag, my lord. I'm sure you'll find one up to your weight.'

Farmer was also helpful in directing Noah onto a shorter path back into town.

He was a little surprised at how near the house was to the town and surmised the property was not as extensive as he had been led to believe. His return route, through the stable yard and past various outhouses, opened directly into the town centre. His hotel was also nearby, an ancient inn opposite an imposing church.

He found Bill in their rooms, studying his reading lessons. Noah had started them during the less turbulent periods of their voyage and Bill proved to be a fast learner.

'How'd it go?' Bill asked, packing away his books.

Noah sat down and started to pull off his long boots. 'I'm not sure. There are so many contradictions. The estate is quite small.' He gave a short laugh. 'So is Mrs Laing. She looks fragile but I sense a coil of steel that she was trying to hide behind small talk and fine manners. We will move in tomorrow and see how the land really lies.'

'Well,' Hattie demanded as soon as she had given her cloak and bonnet to Pound.

Lois raised an eyebrow and led the way to the small parlour she preferred to the more formal rooms. Once the door was closed, she sat down and sighed. 'Oh, Hattie, I don't know what to make of him. He is not as uncouth as I expected.'

'Where is he?'

'He has returned to his hotel for the night and will come back tomorrow.'

Hattie gave a huff of annoyance. 'But what does he look like? I only had a brief glimpse as he rode past. Come on, I want to hear all about it.'

Lois's jumbled recollections carried them through dinner. She had no answer to many of Hattie's questions. Beyond his physical appearance and the fact that he was educated, he had given little away. 'He actually owns a sheep farm,' Lois commented.

'Well, that's a start.'

'And he is travelling with a companion. Again, no details. What am I going to do with him?' Lois shook her head. 'He is not a guest but, at present, he has no authority.'

'And you are quite taken with him,' Hattie said with a wink.

'No, no! It is just... Oh, I don't know.'

Hattie nodded. 'If you say so. I've not seen you so flustered since.... well, not ever.'

It was true. Lois was not given to emotion. Oh, she laughed when amused and sympathised with the less fortunate, but she lived her life on an even keel, taking each situation as it came and dealing with it as seemed appropriate.

Hattie left soon after, leaving Lois with her thoughts and prayers for guidance on how to behave tomorrow.

Chapter 3

Noah took Lois by surprise next morning. Given his apparent disinterest both before and after he'd landed in England, Lois did not expect his arrival any time soon. She was lingering over her breakfast when she heard his voice in the hall. It was barely nine o'clock! Why did he always catch her on the wrong foot?

Lois put down her unfinished tea and went to meet him. Her greeting froze on her lips at the sight of his companion. Even in new clothes, Bill did not look like a gentleman.

Noah was hard put not to laugh at her opened-mouthed surprise. 'This is Bill Norton, my friend and saviour.'

It seemed a strange introduction. The grinning giant at his side touched a finger to his hat, then swiftly pulled it off. He seemed unsure what to do with it and finally tucked the hat under his arm. 'Ma'am,' he muttered into the folds of his neck-scarf, and his face darkened to an unbecoming red.

Lord Laing did not appear to notice anything wrong. 'Will someone, please, show Bill to our quarters?' Bill took that as a signal to move and turned to grab a couple of the bags he had dropped by the door.

'Someone will see to your baggage, sir,' Pound said, more in control of the situation than Lois. 'If you will follow me.'

Lois snapped out of her trance. 'I will show His Lordship the way,' she said, managing to conjure a small smile. 'I think a tour of the house would be a good place to start his induction.' That was wrong! It made him sound like a trainee footman. But it was said now and Lois covered her confusion by indicating the wide staircase.

'The master suite is at the front of the house. The last baron liked to see who was approaching. You may choose another room if you wish. There are seventeen bedrooms, not counting the servants' quarters.' Now she had started talking, Lois did not seem able to stop. She was quite out of breath by the time they reached the first floor, and she turned right onto an opened corridor.

Noah paused and turned to look down into the main hall. It was square and not very large considering the impression from outside. Its half-panelled walls were punctuated by wide doors with ornate frames. Above the panelling, the walls were painted a soft yellow that seemed to bring the sunshine into what would otherwise have been an oppressive space. Looking up, Noah could see a second gallery around three sides of the next floor. Higher above the walls were windows and a domed ceiling.

Lois had regained her breath. The stairs had taken them away from the front door and another flight rose across the back of the landing. Lois turned right and opened the first door. 'This was George's study,' she said, automatically referring to her dead father-in-law by his given name.

Noah did not comment and glanced into the large room. He would explore it later.

'Dressing room,' Lois said as they passed another door. They had reached the end of the passage, and the next door facing them had double leaves with a deeply carved frame. The handles and hinges gleamed like gold from years of polishing. Lois opened one of the doors and Noah stepped forward to push the other one. After such an impressive portal, the room was not what Noah would have expected. It was certainly large, with windows on two sides, but there was no grandeur. A curtainless, four-poster bed stood isolated in a sea of speckled grey carpet. Around the wall were various dark oak cabinets. A large armchair stood by the uncurtained window. Apart from a portrait of a youngish woman above the fireplace, the room was bare of ornament.

'I did not know your taste in furnishing,' Lois commented to explain the bareness. 'I have a selection of draperies laid out for you to choose from and, of course, you may have any furniture that takes your fancy.'

'I am not a very fancy man,' Noah reassured her. 'Some plain curtains and a table beside the bed would be useful. So too would a table and upright chairs.'

As they turned to leave, Noah noticed another door. 'What's through there?'

'It was the baroness's suite.'

'You don't use it?'

'Certainly not! I have a suite in the west wing.' As she did not offer any further information, Noah asked, 'Where have you put Bill?'

'You did not tell me the status of your companion. I will show you the rest of the rooms and you can decide.' There was a slight note of censure in her tone and Noah realised he had been at fault. The English upper classes were very particular. A person of rank would be given a better room than a mere servant. Bill was neither. 'Bill is my friend and guest. I am sure he will be treated as such.'

Before Lois could reply, Bill, who had been silently trailing them, commented, 'Somewhere a bit cosier than this. Reminds me of the barracks!'

Noah had crossed to the windows and saw that what he had been shown so far was only the protruding section of the house. One of the wings stretched away to his left and before him was the approach road flanked by formal gardens. Beyond them was the high stone wall, but over it he could see the church tower and it made him feel that they were part of the town.

Lois took them back to the landing and opened a door Noah had not previously noticed. It opened onto a wide corridor lit by large windows at the far end. Lois said, 'This is the east wing.' She glanced at Bill. 'Bachelors are traditionally housed here or married couples if we have many guests.'

'Do you entertain often?' Noah asked.

'Not recently. George lost his heart for company towards the end.' Lois did not need to add more as her sorrow was obvious. He would find out how recent that loss was at a later date.

Door after door was opened for their perusal. The bedrooms were all similar in size, with a single window and heavy furniture, mostly shrouded in dust sheets. Bill was asked to make his choice.

'Any will do. It's only for sleeping.'

'There is a staircase at the end that leads to the next floors.' Lois tilted her head and there was a note of enquiry in her voice as though to ask if they wanted to proceed.

'I think we have seen enough bedrooms for now,' Noah decided. As they retraced their steps, Lois suggested Mr Norton use the room nearest the stairs, and the men nodded.

Lois hesitated when they reached the start of the west wing. 'More bedrooms. My apartments are down there.' She did not offer to show them but quickly made her way back down the stairs. Pound was hovering in the hall with a footman and the baggage.

'Mr Norton will use the Milton room,' Lois told him before explaining to Noah that all the rooms had names, to which Noah added, 'More personal than numbers.'

'Yes. It equalises things. The master suite would be number one and a visitor might feel slighted at being given number sixteen!' It was the most natural statement she had yet offered, and Noah liked the change. So far, she had sounded like a professional guide.

'Do you wish to continue the tour or stop for coffee?' Noah had to stifle a laugh at the return of the starchy guide. 'Coffee, please.' Perhaps refreshment would continue the softening process.

They were served their drinks in a large room on the ground floor. It was pleasantly furnished with lighter furniture, the walls papered and with pictures and ornaments to make it more lived in. A bright fire burned in the wide hearth and the windows overlooked more gardens. Lois and Noah sat on either side of the fire, but Bill chose a seat near the window.

It was a replay of yesterday, no one inclined to open a conversation. Noah hoped Mrs Laing would not always be so starchy. Women did not usually freeze in his presence and, without being vain, he recalled the many lures cast his way.

Their coffee was served and Noah asked, 'What is my next lesson to be?'

Lois laughed softly. 'Have I been acting like a schoolteacher?' She sighed. 'This is difficult for me. You are the baron but George left me with the responsibility of ensuring Laington's future care.'

'You were very fond of the baron?'

Lois smiled. 'He was like a father to me. I have lived here since I was six years old and love the estate as much as he did.'

'And your husband?'

Lois stiffened. 'Yes.' Her tone dared him to continue.

There was a short silence until Lois asked if he was ready to continue the tour.

'I would prefer to take a walk outside. To get my bearings.'

Bill Norton surged to his feet. 'We could take a look at the flock,' he said eagerly.

'They have not yet been brought down for lambing,' Lois told him. 'Perhaps tomorrow you might ride out to see them.' The big man's disappointment was obvious and Lois suggested, 'But you could see the stables.' She paused to give him an assessing glance. 'I am not sure we have anything up to your weight,' she continued dubiously.

Noah indicated a portrait of a large black horse displayed on one of the walls.

Lois shook her head. 'Jupiter was sold.' It was another conversation stopper and Noah wondered how many other subjects were taboo.

'Today we will just acquaint ourselves with the house and grounds,' Noah decided and raised his hand when Lois also got to her feet. 'There is no need for you to show us. We won't get lost.' His smile softened his refusal and did strange things to Lois's stomach.

She watched the men leave with a feeling of relief. She had been surrounded by men all her life but never before had felt so unsure of herself. Giving an annoyed shake of her shoulders, Lois went to attend to the refurbishment of their rooms.

As the men headed for the stables, Bill gave Noah a sly look. 'You'll have trouble charming that one.'

'I don't want to charm her,' Noah replied harshly. Ruthlessly squashing a twinge of doubt, he moderated his tone and quickened his pace, saying, over his shoulder, 'I won't be staying so there is no point in trying.'

Young Tommy was sweeping the stable yard and, at their approach, he dropped his broom and ran into the tack room calling, 'Pa! The young master's coming!'

The stable master came out to meet them. 'Good morning, my lord. Can I show you around?' A stern nod to his son prevented the boy from coming into the stable with them.

Everything was clean and well kept. The aroma of fresh hay overlaid the ingrained smell of confined horses, some of whom poked their heads over the half doors.

Noah counted four. Not many for a supposedly large estate. 'The carriage horses and a pregnant mare are out in the paddock,' Farmer informed him, going to the end loose box. 'Perhaps you would like to take a closer look at Sampson.' While he spoke, Farmer had unlatched the door and deftly clipped a lead rein onto the huge gelding's bridle. 'He's a bit fresh,' Farmer warned at Bill instantly went towards the horse.

He need not have worried. With a soft murmur, Bill held out his hand and the horse nickered in replay and bent his head.

Farmer handed Bill the lead and spoke quietly to Noah. 'He has a way with horses,' he commented in approval.

'All creatures,' Noah assured him. He watched Bill lead the large horse outside before asking, 'Do you have anything suitable for me? That one appears to be taken.'

'Juno might suit, for the time being,' Farmer suggested dubiously. 'The mistress doesn't ride much.' He looked sideways at Noah. 'Do you mind a mare?'

Juno proved to be a fine animal with a white star on her forehead. She looked strong but docile and, as he did not intend to be here long, Noah said she would do.

Noah left Bill happily discussing horses with Farmer and began his circuit of the house. With the recent tour of the interior fresh in his mind, he was better able to judge the real scale of the house. Given the number of windows, he guessed the ground floor rooms to be less numerous and larger in size than the bedrooms. The driveway ended at the stables but a paved path continued along the side of the east wing, past various service buildings. At the corner, the path widened into a terrace with another, lesser drive snaking away behind the stables.

A cart was drawn up close to the doorway and two men were unloading what looked like sacks of vegetables. They touched their caps as Noah passed. He felt their eyes on his back and caught low, indecipherable conversation – no doubt about him. It was to be expected and Noah wondered just how many staff were employed. He chuckled to himself. He had caught Mrs Laing out again. Had she known the time of his arrival, the whole workforce would have been lined up to greet him. Thank goodness he had been spared that embarrassment!

The rear of the house presented a totally different aspect. The high wall was much closer here and the ground paved the whole way. He could not guess its function as it was totally barren. The wing was divided in the centre by a pair of wide and tall doors. Looking up, he could see mismatched windows and a variety of finishes. It was as though the architect had lost interest in design and used any materials available. With a shrug, he continued to the next corner.

The western side of the house came as a surprise. The terrace had a carved stone balustrade and wide steps dropped to a series of lawns, gardens with statuary and parkland beyond. Small stands of mature trees dotted the park, adding interest, along with what Noah knew were called follies – picturesque but useless buildings.

He turned his attention back to the house. Most of the ground-floor windows were either low to the ground or glazed doors. He could imagine the rooms within inhabited by finely dressed gentry who could easily step outside to admire the view.

The view was equally available to the upper rooms' inhabitants by the addition of convenient balconies. Noah did not know a great deal about British architecture but Laington Manor seemed as complicated as its present mistress.

Finally completing his circuit of the house at the front door, Noah tried to assess how he felt about owning it. It was certainly intriguing to think generation after generation of his forebears had walked these paths. Relatives he had not been aware of until he'd received the summons. Prior to that, Gramp had seldom mentioned his time in England. When pressed for information, he had merely said it was a land ruled by snobbish aristocrats who thought more of their status and possessions than they did of people and he was glad to have been deported.

Noah's father had insisted that the older man, his father, was not a convicted criminal although his devil-may-care, rollicking lifestyle would surely send him to hell.

Hell was Robert Laing's favourite topic. Noah's earliest years had been oppressed by endless prayers, penances and threats of damnation. He had only really started to live when his father died and he came into the, somewhat haphazard, care of his grandfather.

Noah tried to envisage Gramp living here. The arrival of the letters had opened the floodgates, but Gramp's account had been as though he was speaking about someone else. Time and distance could not hide his contempt for a regime he had been glad to leave. How that had come about had amazed and amused Noah, and he wondered how the story would be seen from the English perspective and whether Mrs Laing would be able, or willing, to share the knowledge.

Chapter 4

Lois was being bombarded with questions. Close neighbours, Clive and Irene Grainger, had heard of the new baron's arrival and rushed to be the first to meet him. The pair were similar in colouring and features but where they made Irene look like a pretty, dark-haired doll, they made Clive appear weary and old beyond his twenty-four years.

Irene went straight to the mirror and fussed with her hair. Clive sat beside Lois without invitation and she shifted away. He had been trying to court her since her mourning year was over but was always gently rebuffed. Lois turned sideways, making a little more space between them.

'Where is the new baron?' Irene asked excitedly, not bothering to turn around. 'And who is that monster riding Sampson round the paddock?'

Lois sighed. She had known them for a long time. The girl acted younger than her seventeen years despite the efforts of her mother and governess to teach her ladylike manners. 'Out surveying his property. And there is no need to primp in the mirror, you look perfect as usual.'

'And you will set yourself alight if you move any closer to the fire,' her brother grumbled. 'She would insist on coming with me. But who is the large stranger?'

'I assume you were referring to Mr Norton. He is Lord Laing's travelling companion and guest.'

'Guest!' Irene twittered. 'He looks more like an ogre. I would be afraid to meet him.'

'That is unfortunate if you intend staying for luncheon. Lord Laing insists Mr Norton be treated civilly.'

'Are you still calling him Lord Laing?' Irene faced Lois and tittered. 'How droll. If you want to be a real baroness you had better get closer acquainted.'

'Irene!' Clive and Lois scolded together.

Lois's dislike of the girl rose another notch. She was nothing like her elder sister, Mary, who had been Lois's closest friend until she married and moved away.

'And what is your opinion of Lord Laing, my dear? Has he told you why it took him so long to get here?'

'It is a long journey from Australia,' Lois replied blandly.

'Not two years. And you said he reached London a month ago.'

'I have not enquired into his movements or motives. Besides which, I will not discuss him behind his back!' Lois said with as much disapproval as she could get into her voice. The reproof slid off Clive like water off a du He took hold of Lois's hand. 'Come now, don't be coy. He must have given you some explanation.'

Lois moved to stand by the window. Her stomach was quietly rumbling, reminding her of her interrupted breakfast. She glanced at the clock. It was gone one o'clock. How much longer was it going to take the tiresome man to walk around the house? She moved to the window.

The subject of her thoughts was trying to convince Bill that he did not need to groom the horse. 'Mrs Laing will be expecting us back and you need to change your boots before you go inside.'

Bill looked down at his dusty and dung-encrusted footwear. 'I don't have any others. You made me throw my old ones away,' Bill complained.

'Allow me, sir,' Farmer said. 'If you sit at that barrel, I'll have you house-fit in a trice.'

Noah and Bill's return necessitated introductions and caused a further delay before they could go in to luncheon. When they finally took their seats at the octagonal table laid in the small dining room, three pairs of eyes were slyly focused on Bill. Lois breathed a sigh of relief when he shook out his napkin and laid it tidily in his lap. The soup was served and everyone waited for Lois to pick up her spoon before dipping their own into the fragrant liquid. The meal continued in relative harmony.

Noah had made sure Bill knew what would be expected of him. Polite table manners were easy but he had not succeeded in making Bill converse in anything but monosyllables. The Graingers largely ignored him beyond a few theatrical shudders from Irene, and in their separate ways they tried to extract information from Noah. He did reply with more than a single word, but his answers were bland. It was left to Lois to try to unite the motley group.

When they had finally seen the guests off the property, Lois and Noah returned to the sitting room. Bill had disappeared.

Noah flopped into a chair and ran a finger around his collar. 'My God, I have had more interesting meals with my sheep!'

'Well, you did not help a great deal,' Lois complained.

'They were just being nosy. And that girl should not be allowed out.'

'I hope Mr Norton was not offended.'

'He's endured far worse treatment than a cold shoulder.'

Lois picked up her embroidery. 'Tell me about him.'

The needle rammed into her finger when Noah replied, 'No.'

'I *am not* being nosy! I will be sharing a house with him for the foreseeable future and it helps to make a guest comfortable if you know a little about them.'

'It helps to know a bit about any person you have to spend time with,' Noah challenged.

'Touché,' Lois conceded. It was a fair comment. She knew she had been offhand on several occasions. She laid aside her needlework and got to her feet. 'Will you come to the document room? It will explain why we are in this awkward situation.'

The afternoon light was fading but the corridors were well lit, and Noah was surprised when Lois picked up one of the small lamps from a side table. He offered to carry it as Lois led the way towards the back of the house. They turned a corner, into a darker passage, and Lois opened a door. The room stuck chill after being in the drawing room, but Lois did not suggest lighting the fire ready laid in the hearth. Noah just had time to gain an impression of a smallish room panelled from floor to ceiling and furnished with a large table and upright chairs before Lois requested his help in opening the long shutters.

Noah placed the lamp on the table and reached up to the top bolts while Lois dealt with the bottom. As Lois straightened up, she was caught under Noah's arm and, for a tense second, they stared into each other's eyes before Lois moved away. She opened one of the wall panels to reveal a deep cupboard from which she extracted a rolled document. Noah helped her to unroll and weigh it down on the table with a couple of polished stones.

Noah had never seen a family tree, but it was not too dissimilar to the stud charts he was familiar with.

Lois was already pointing out that there were few side branches, all except Noah's having died out long ago. His eyes went immediately to the bottom of the list, where his name appeared.

Lois drew his attention to the first entry. 'The estate and title were gifted to Augustus Laing in 1667 by King Charles as a reward for his support.'

Lois had a clear, pleasant voice that prevented her tale sounding like a lecture. Noah was content to listen as she explained that Augustus had posed as a Republican while secretly sending money to the exiled King.

'His wife, Marie, was Flemish and bravely carried the gold to the Continent when she visited her family. As a reward, the King gave her a small plot to be held exclusively by females so it never became part of the main estate. It is called Laington Grace.'

'Now occupied by Miss Brown. Is she another relative?'

Lois laughed. 'No. She was the last Lady Laing's maid. Lady Charlotte's last wish was that Hattie live at Laington Grace and be a comfort to George.'

'How comforting?'

Lois pokered up. 'That is her business. She will be coming to dinner so you may ask her yourself.'

Lois went back to being an instructor. Her tone soon softened to a quiet pride as though she was relating her own history.

Nothing significant seemed to have happened for the next hundred and fifty years. The family prospered and increased their holdings. 'We still have a strong connection to the wool trade,' she commented before touching an entry close to the bottom of the roll.

'Here we have your branch. The eleventh baron had three sons who all predeceased him. Arthur, your great-grandfather, was the youngest and had a twin sister, Ashley.' Lois looked up. 'Please stop me if I am telling you things you already know.'

'Please carry on. Gramp rarely spoke of the past.' Noah was interested to learn how much of Gramp's life was known in England.

Lois continued. 'The twins seem to have disappeared when they were seventeen or eighteen. There is no evidence that the baron tried to find them or bring them back.' She looked at Noah enquiringly and he saw no harm in telling her, 'They joined a travelling theatre company.'

'Ah, that fits. We do know that Arthur became a playwriter and Ashley was a singer, using the name Gloria Morrow.' Lois paused to see if Noah had more to add. They were getting close to facts that really interested Noah, and he suggested they sit down.

Lois moved a stone and the parchment slowly re-rolled itself. She seemed reluctant to continue.

'Do you know why Ernest left?' Noah asked.

Lois sighed. 'He was wild. An inveterate gambler, drinker and into any mischief he could find.'

'He never changed,' Noah said with a laugh. 'But he was immensely likeable and I was very fond of him.'

'So was George. Ernest was much older and although they did not spend much time together, George admired his independent nature. But you will know that.'

Noah did not answer directly. 'I did not know Gramp had a brother until the baron's letter arrived. Please continue.'

Lois looked surprised and it took her a moment to recall where she had got to. Noah listened, patching the details into Gramp's disjointed account.

Ernest had been eleven years old and George about four when their father brought them to England. The age gap and years at school kept them apart and they were reputed to be totally different in character. 'George was at school when Ernest was sent away. He was only told that Ernest had finally crossed the line of decency when he ran away with a married woman. He said Ernest wrote for a while then they lost all contact.'

Noah nodded. 'He always laughingly said he was deported. What details I know are the memories of a tired old man.'

They fell silent, each thinking of the old men who had been important to them.

'So, there you have it,' Lois finally commented. 'George was afraid you would follow in your grandfather's footsteps and squander the estate he had tried so hard to protect.'

A gong sounded in the distance and Lois got to her feet. 'That is the dressing gong. We usually dine early unless there are guests. You may change things to suit yourself, of course.'

'Without your permission?'

'Lord Laing, you are the baron. I am just a custodian.' Lois was already on her way to the door, saying over her shoulder, 'Your rooms have been prepared. Please excuse me.'

Noah did not rush after her. He went to the window but it was now quite dark and he could not see beyond his reflection in the glass. He wondered if he should close the shutters, but a footman arrived to attend to them and dowse the lamp. The corridors and stairs in the main section of the house were well lit at intervals and Noah had no trouble finding his way.

When he reached the room allocated to Bill, he paused. He had completely forgotten about his friend and wondered what he had been doing all afternoon. He knocked on the door and entered without waiting for a reply. Bill was sitting on the side of the bed looking completely lost.

'Thank God you've come,' Bill grumbled. 'I have been told to dress for dinner. What's wrong with this?' A sweep of his hand indicated the smart suit Noah had purchased for him. It was rather rumpled but otherwise similar to the other two someone had hung in the huge wardrobe.

Noah went to the wardrobe and pulled out the black suit and tossed it onto the bed. 'And change your shirt and wear a white cravat.'

'What a load of fuss! We didn't have to change at any of the hotels we stayed in.'

'We dined in our rooms,' Noah explained patiently. 'Now you will be dining in style with two ladies. Get changed.'

Noah found his own room had been transformed. A lamp on the mantlepiece showed drapes in shades of red and brown had been hung round the bed and at the windows. They added warmth to the room, as did the fire burning brightly behind a mesh screen. Several pictures adorned the walls and books had been placed on a table close to the bed.

In the dressing room he found his luggage had been unpacked and stowed away. His shaving gear was laid out on a marble-topped washstand with a mirror above. A large copper jug of hot water was keeping warm close to another small fire. He was unused to such pampering. At home he used the communal bathhouse or carried his own water up to his room. He never had a fire up there, even in winter. What comforts he required were supplied by his elderly housekeeper.

Noah felt sudden sympathy for Bill, who was completely out of his element. But it had been unthinkable to leave him in London waiting for news of the long-lost brother they had discovered.

It did not take Noah long to ready himself for dinner, and he went along to check on Bill. The big man had spruced himself up and even shaved, but he was still far from appearing a gentleman.

'What do we do now?' Bill asked.

'We wait for another gong to tell us when to go down.'

Bill muttered something unintelligible and Noah tried to distract him by asking where he had been all afternoon. The change in Bill's demeanour was instant. 'I went walkabout. There's more to this place than meets the eye. I didn't find any sheep but there are cows, hens, dogs and more horses.'

Noah heard how Bill had encountered numerous workers who made him feel welcome and were very informative. 'They are all full of praise for the old man and Mrs Laing. They tried to find out about you, but I didn't say nothing.' Bill was still rambling on about gardens and even a hothouse when another gong echoed through the building.

The men were met at the bottom of the stairs by Pound, who directed them to the drawing room. 'I thought we were going to dinner,' Bill muttered. 'I'm starved.'

In the drawing room, Lois and Hattie were discussing the newcomers. Lois had no qualms about sharing her views with Hattie. Her opinions would go no further and would receive sensible advice. They stopped when the men entered the room.

'This is Miss Harriet Brown, my lord,' Lois introduced formally.

'There's no need for that, love.' Hattie moved forward, holding out her hand. 'I'm Hattie. I called George by his name and I'll call you Noah.' She turned to the big man lingering in the doorway. 'And you'll be Bill. Don't stand there! I don't bite!'

Although she was richly dressed, Hattie was more the kind of woman Bill was accustomed to. They spoke straight and bowed to no man.

The party fell into natural pairs. Lois offered drinks and was glad she had ordered ale, which was Bill's choice. Noah smiled at Lois and sat opposite her while the other two cosied up a short distance away.

'I knew Hattie would be able to put Mr Norton at ease. I hope she did not offend you.'

'Not at all. If she is to call me Noah, might you try to do the same? I am not used to this lordship business.'

'And I am Lois.' The ice was broken but neither felt ready to start a conversation. Instead, they looked fondly at their friends until Hattie gave them a saucy wink.

'How do the locals react to Hattie? Bill went exploring and said he was well received.'

'Hattie does not try to join the higher levels of society, but she is not shunned. She is a member of the local charity group and helps at the school we hold here. She shares outing with me. We shop and attend church together. Some of the sticklers tut but she has never been insulted that I know of.'

Pound appeared to call them into dinner.

The dining room was enough to make Bill stare open-mouthed. Pictures adorned the red plush walls, the most imposing being a large portrait of a seated king in full regalia.

Silver-laden sideboards surrounded a long table. Lois had ordered most of the leaves be removed and the spare chairs pushed back to the walls, but it was still long enough to accommodate ten or twelve people. Knowing how Hattie would react to formality, Lois had the seating arranged at one end. She gently manoeuvred Noah towards the head of the table, taking her place on his right with Hattie and Bill on his left.

The meal started decorously but, by the time the covers were removed, they were all chatting away merrily.

Lois gained more insight into Noah's background than would have been gained by direct questions. The journey Noah had described briefly as horrendous, Bill made sound like an adventure. 'Noah was sicker than a poisoned dingo,' he confided. 'I thought he'd turn himself inside out.'

'Too graphic,' Noah commented.

'I don't know what that means but I think I've been told to shut up,' Bill replied, making them laugh.

Pound and the attending footmen but hard put not to join in.

The light atmosphere continued until Hattie announced it was past her bedtime. Bill disappeared at the same time, leaving Lois and Noah alone.

'Your friend is quite a character,' Noah said with a smile.

'So too is yours. I would never have guessed he could be so witty.'

'I think the wine helped. And there are unplumbed depths to Bill. Some of the things he came out with were a revelation to me.'

Lois silently recalled that Noah had given little away, being more intent on boosting Bill's confidence. She wasn't so at ease now and sought for some neutral topic.

Noah saved her the effort. 'I should like to go further afield tomorrow. Farmer has suggested I ride Juno, who I believe is your usual mount.'

Lois answered the unspoken query by assuring him that she preferred to use the pony trap.

'Don't you like riding?'

Lois looked sad and repeated her previous statement.

Another dead end, Noah thought. Despite his intention not to get involved, Noah found himself spending far too much time wondering about Lois. The use of her given name seemed to have heightened his curiosity. His perusal of the family tree had been too brief to note when she had married or how long she had been a widow. He knew it was common for middle-aged men to take young wives, but it made her a tragically young widow.

Lois filled the sudden silence by suggesting the route they would take tomorrow. Added details carried them through until Lois retired.

Nosh resumed his seat after she left. It had been a full but not particularly active day, and he was not ready for bed. He felt restless and got up to wander around the room, examining curios in glass-fronted cases and the pictures on the wall. He wondered about the black horse and resolved to ask Farmer why it had been sold. Moving on, he paused at the sideboard, considered, then rejected, the idea of pouring himself another brandy from the cut glass decanter. With a huff of frustration, he decided so go up to his room and see what kind of books Lois thought would interest him.

Chapter 5

Noah awoke later than usual next morning. It had taken him a long time to get to sleep when he eventually reached his room.

As he had exited the drawing room, another, older, footman had risen from the hooded porter's chair by the front door and hastily tucked away the newspaper he had been reading. They nodded to each other but did not speak. Noah suspected it was the man's duty to wait for everyone to go to bed before he secured the house for the night. Not that he could envisage anyone breaking in.

On a whim he decided to explore the other ground-floor rooms and crossed the hall to the opposite door. It was dark inside so he turned back to pick up a lamp that stood, ready lit, on a table. The footman eyed him curiously but Noah remembered that this was his house. He could go wherever he liked without permission or explanation. He firmly closed the door behind him and looked around. It was another large sitting room. The curtains were closed and the air had the chill of a seldom-used space. A fire was laid in the hearth ready to be lit if required. It was the first sign of economy he had seen. Lamps burned in every passage and fires were lit in his quarters well ahead of the time he could be expected to use them. The dinner had been of several courses, each with a choice of wine, and they had been served tea and unnecessary biscuits before Hattie left.

Instead of returning to the hall, he opened another door at the side of the room. It led into what Noah supposed had been George's study. No, Lois had said that was upstairs, next to the dressing room. But it was obviously a working space with a large desk and drawer cabinets. There was a map on the wall which he examined closer. The house was depicted close to the bottom right-hand borders. To the left and upwards it showed buildings, fields, woodlands and roads. Noah did a rough calculation. If the map was drawn to scale, the estate really was larger than he had thought. He whistled softly. It was a hell of a lot for one young woman to oversee.

He left by another door into what appeared to be another, smaller, office. It was not as spartan and had a comfortable sitting area near the fireplace. Noah sensed this was where Lois spent much of her time and it made him feel like an intruder.

She intrigued him and he wanted to know why she had such an intense attachment to Laington. Perhaps another look at the family tree would tell him more.

He continued his exploration towards the back of the house. A door behind the staircase opened into a corridor that branched left and right, blocked a little way along by double-leaved doors. Straight ahead, another passage was dimly lit at intervals. Noah ventured a few steps. Rough carpet beneath his feet, walls lined with glass-fronted cabinets and a faint smell of cooking, suggestive of a kitchen, made him turn back.

He retraced his steps to the junction and his mental map told him the left-hand passage would lead into the western wing. The décor on the other side of the door confirmed his reasoning. It was well lit. The floor covering was soft and pictures hung between the doors. He glanced into several rooms but did not find the one he was looking for.

He reached another junction that branched right and left. Ahead of him was the dining room. He had lost his bearings, and his interest in exploring further dissipated.

The hallway had been empty when he returned to his starting point and he wondered how the footman would know when to douse the lamps. With a shrug he left his lamp on the hall table and climbed the stairs.

Loud snores came from behind Bill's bedroom door as he past and he felt a twinge of guilt at leaving his friend to his own devices. Bill was a fish out of water and could quite easily cause offence by breaching the rules of etiquette Noah had not had the time nor thought to teach him.

Sleep was a long time coming as he lay in bed trying to order the many discoveries made that day. When he had finally fallen asleep, his dreams had been of the past he had left behind.

Chapter 6

Lois awoke at her usual time next morning, just as her maid, Sarah, entered with the early morning tea. Lois sat on the side of the bed to drink, casting her eyes over the list of tasks she had made before going to sleep. She had a lot to do before Noah came down and was determined not to be caught out again.

Sarah had opened the curtains and retired to the dressing room. She was in her late fifties, small and quick in her movements. Sarah had cared for Lois since she had come to Laington as a small child. They shared the mutual ease and affection of long acquaintance. Their relationship had changed over the years with Sarah gradually relinquishing control and instilling in Lois a respect for the subtle line, neither servile nor condescending, that ought to exist between mistress and servant.

Lois finished her tea and went to get dressed. With their proposed outing in mind, she chose a serviceable outfit of grey skirt and blouse. A matching jacket would be added later.

Several hours later, Lois was growing impatient. She had already had her daily meetings with the cook and housekeeper and arranged for Pound to assemble the staff to meet the baron when he deigned to appear. Yesterday Noah had arrived from town before nine o'clock and she had expected him to come down long ago.

Bill Norton had appeared shortly after seven, sheepishly enquiring if it was time for breakfast. Lois had sat with him, idly toying with a piece of toast, while he devoured a huge plate of eggs, bacon and potato washed down with cup after cup of black tea. Beyond acknowledging that he had slept well, he was back into his silent shell.

Bill's breakfast had been cleared and the chaffing dishes refreshed and there was still no sign of Noah. Lois was not going to waste any more time and went to her office, leaving the door open. She was immersed in one of the farm reports when she heard Noah descend the stairs. Lois stepped out into the hall to meet him.

'Good morning,' he greeted her cheerfully. 'Am I too late for breakfast?'

'You may eat at whatever time you choose, my lord. It would be a help to the kitchen if they had some idea of your preferred timetable.'

Ho, ho, Noah thought. *I'm in trouble again.*

He followed Lois into the small dining room they had used for lunch yesterday and helped himself from the heated dishes on the sideboard. The eggs were still soft and the bacon un-shrivelled so the staff were either mind-readers or someone had been keeping tabs on his movements. His last thought was confirmed when a maid suddenly appeared with fresh toast and asked if he preferred tea or coffee.

'Will you join me?' Noah asked Lois. 'Or have you already eaten?'

Lois gave a nod that could have applied to either statement and gratefully served herself a portion of eggs and toast. She poured the tea when it arrived and commented that Mr Norton had declined milk.

Noah put down his cutlery. 'Lois, please bear with us. Bill's life has been devoid of such luxuries. All this' – he waved his hand vaguely – 'is unfamiliar territory. I have been educated, moved in society, etc, but I work as hard as any of my men. My home is comfortable but lacking all the frills and rules you take for granted. Bill was a transportee who has served his sentence. He was working his passage back to England and cared for me when I might have died of seasickness. We will make mistakes but your life will go back to normal once we leave.'

The tea in Lois's cup slopped onto the table. 'Leave! But you can't! What will happen to Laington?'

It struck Noah that she'd referred to the estate as though it was a living entity. He shrugged. 'I had thought to dispose of it.' He frowned. 'That was before I was told you are in charge. Are you finding it too much? It was unfair of George to suddenly place so much responsibility on your shoulders.'

Lois had calmed down and mopped the spilt tea before it could trickle off the edge of the table. 'It was not sudden. George had been training me for years. Oh, not to take over the whole estate but Simon abhorred bookwork and preferred to be out and about, doing things.' She stopped abruptly. In her shock she had opened the way to explanations she had been dreading. She turned the conversation away from herself. 'Towards the end, George was hanging all his hopes on you to eventually take over and produce an heir.'

Noah felt a sudden tightness in his chest. The situation evoked memories but also obliged him to be more open. 'I am sorry I did not meet him. My circumstance made it impossible for me to come immediately. Then things happened and I needed a change.'

It sounded a very poor excuse and gave no hint of the tragedy and trauma he had been through.

Lois sensed a deep sadness in her companion. It echoed her own. There were still things to be told but, at this moment, they were both too vulnerable to continue.

She stood up. 'Well, while you are here, I suggest we behave as would be expected. A lot of people depend on Laington's stability.' She was at the door before Noah realised he was supposed to follow. There was the sound of movement in the hall, rustling and footsteps. By the time he joined Lois in the doorway, the staff had arranged themselves in lines of rank and gender.

'Lord Laing, I belatedly introduce your staff.'

She did not do it personally. Pound named and outlined the duties of the two footmen and outdoor staff. Noah counted eighteen, including young Tommy.

Lois introduced the housekeeper, Mrs Collins, a stern, middle-aged woman who took over to introduce the females, starting with a woman who bore a striking resemblance to Hattie. 'Mrs Brown is our highly valued cook.'

The woman bobbed a curtsey. She had a confident manner and said, 'I am Hattie's twin sister. It used to cause no end of laughs when we first came here.'

Mrs Collins frowned and moved down the line. Lois's maid appeared quite elderly and the other maids very young. He did not try to remember all the names. But he had witnessed this kind of event and knew what was expected of him. Taking his place beside Lois, he addressed the company. 'I thank you for your welcome. I am sure I will receive the same loyal service you rendered to the late baron and, more recently, to Mrs Laing. I will not keep you from your work any longer.' He ended with a nod to Pound and Mrs Collins and turned away. He had no idea where he was supposed to go but Lois's proximity obliged him to move with her into the smaller of the offices he had discovered.

'Well done,' Lois said approvingly after she had closed the door. 'To the manor born, one might say.'

Noah laughed. 'I told you I was not completely uncivilised. What do we do now?'

In the daylight he could see the room in more detail and noted the feminine touches he had only sensed the night before. As well as the armchairs on either side of the fireplace, there was a sewing table and delicate watercolour pictures on the walls.

'This is where I see the managers,' Lois explained. She laughed at his look of surprise. 'I am not alone. We have reliable managers for each section. I receive their personal reports on a regular schedule. Where their duties overlap and for general overviews we meet in the main office' – she indicated the side door – 'or in another sitting room.'

It echoed his own regime, although he generally met his foremen outside.

Lois continued. 'I thought today you might like to see more of the estate. We can't cover everything but, if Bill comes with us, he can get to see the sheep he has been hankering for.'

It was soon arranged and the trio set out, the men riding and Lois in her pony trap. They went first to the home farm. More new names and faces. Everything looked orderly and well cared for. The manager was deferential but confident.

As they progressed further afield, Lois pointed out various features and gave a brief resume of their next port of call. At every stop Lois was greeted as a friend and besieged by the children. So too was Bill. The adults assumed he was a servant, more or less ignored beyond a brief nod. The children stared but seemed unafraid of his size and dark visage. Within moments they had drawn him away to view their part of the world.

At midday they were given refreshments at one of the more distant farms and it was late afternoon by the time they returned to the manor.

Pound greeted them with the information that there had been several callers who had left their cards and who hoped to meet the new baron soon.

'That was the next thing I was going to tell you,' Lois said as they climbed the stairs to their rooms. 'Laington is very much a part of the local community and I thought an informal reception would be a good way for you to meet your more prominent neighbours.'

Noah groaned. 'Are they all like the Graingers?'

Lois tried to suppress a smile. 'Happily not. I know they can be trying but most of our neighbours are less tedious and obviously keen to meet you.' She gave him a sideways look. 'I have to tell you that Bill has invoked a lot of interest. I heard he went exploring on his own yesterday. How will he react to a fairly large gathering?'

Noah considered this. 'He will be uncomfortable and gravitate towards the most vulnerable person present. He will not embarrass you.'

Lois and Noah dined alone as Bill had been invited to Hattie's. The meal was not as convivial as the previous evening, but they were beginning to understand personal limits and spent most of the time discussing the estate, the town and general topics, social and political. The hour they spent in the drawing room touched on their views of society, comparing and finding common ground from both hemispheres. Noah was disappointed when Lois chose to end the evening before ten o'clock.

Chapter 7

The next day followed a long-established pattern. The managers came in the morning, seven of them in all, together with the estate secretary, a youngish man by the name of Hemmings. They met in the east drawing room and stayed on for refreshments when Lois and Noah were called away to meet visitors.

The first to arrive was the vicar, a young, earnest man who hoped to see Noah at church on Sunday. He did not seem offended when Noah told him he was not much of a church goer.

The vicar was ousted by the Mayor of Stapleton, the local town, his wife and two daughters.

Noah liked the middle-aged man who was dignified without being pompous. He was less taken with the Mayoress and her overdressed daughters. He was aware that the girls were being displayed for the post of Baroness, but they were too young, even if he had been in the market for a wife.

The final caller was John Partridge, who introduced himself as a long-time friend. He was about Noah's age or possibly older, with pleasant but unremarkable features. His familiarity was not as cloying as Grainger's, but Noah detected an interest in Lois that went beyond mere friendliness. It annoyed Noah that he did not particularly like the idea of Lois having suitors.

John joined them for lunch and, before he left, invited Noah to join him one evening to meet some of the younger people.

'We were thinking of an informal reception here,' Lois said. She waited for Noah's nod before adding, 'I will get the invitations out as soon as possible.'

After he had gone, Lois said, 'You will meet lots of people after church on Sunday. If you choose to attend, that is.'

'I am not much given to religion. My father was a zealous preacher who rammed his views down every throat, mostly mine. I believe it was a reaction to Ernest's free and easy lifestyle.' Noah smiled. 'My grandfather was a reprobate. He lived life to the full until the day he died. It is ironic that it was my father who was killed in a pub, interfering in a drunken brawl. I sometimes think he must be very lonely in Heaven, having consigned most of humanity to Hell.'

Lois should have been shocked at such a candid description of his father, but her own had no claims to sainthood.

Tit for tat, Lois told him her own father had gambled away his fortune, leaving her and her mother destitute. 'That was when George took us in.'

Noah was aware that that was not the whole story, but it had been given voluntarily and he was not about to send her into retreat by asking questions.

Lois wandered over to the window. The weather had turned to heavy rain, making an outdoor tour uninviting. 'I hope it clears by tomorrow,' she said, moving back to the fire. 'It is market day tomorrow and I usually go into town to admire the stalls and catch up on the news.'

'That will please Bill. Not the gossip, but he is more at ease with animals.'

'Oh, I am sorry. Tomorrow is just general stalls and small produce. The stock market is held on alternate Wednesdays on the far side of town. Apparently, years before my time, people started to object to the mess it made in the centre of town and it was relocated.'

Noah guessed that was sometime in the last century. From what he had seen, the buildings edging the wide space, long rather than square, in front of the church were not particularly ancient. New development tended to alter ideas. He had seen it happen in Australia as the shanty towns where cleared and permanent new buildings erected. The new occupants were wealthier and expected cleaner streets.

He sighed. 'Well, I suppose it must be back to the classroom.'

'Are you really finding it tiresome? I thought you would be agog to find out about your inheritance.' Lois paused and frowned. 'Did you really mean it about not remaining here?'

She looked so worried Noah felt a pang of guilt. 'You have to understand that I already have a home and responsibilities.'

'How big is your farm?'

'I don't know exactly. Where you speak of acres I tend to think in square miles.'

Lois was beginning to think they had been deceived. The investigator employed by George to trace his relatives had merely written that Ernest and his grandson were working on a sheep farm. It had taken over a year of exchanged letters to learn even that much. Lois now suspected the search had been cursory to say the least. It also explained why Noah had not seemed impressed or interested in anything beyond his grandfather's early life.

She did not know what to say.

Noah said, 'Sorry,' with genuine sympathy. His own preconceived ideas had also been turned on their heads. Given the fact that he was two generations below the last baron, he had been expecting a middle-aged or even elderly widow completely out of her depth. He had imagined it would be easy to settle her with a pension and dispose of a crumbling estate and a title that held little meaning.

'I could show you the rest of the house,' Lois suggested. To lighten the atmosphere, she added, 'There are more interesting features than bedrooms.'

It would be something to fill the time. Noah nodded his agreement, unaware that Lois had an ulterior motive. Laington might not be the size of his sheep farm, but it was steeped in history. Perhaps awareness of his roots and ancestry would convince Noah to stay.

'I took a look round before I went to bed the other night.' Noah recalled something that had been intriguing him. 'What is that little kitchen next to the dining room used for?'

'It is a serving room. The kitchens are on the other side of the house and the food used to get cold. I persuaded George to create a service area where it is kept warm until needed.' Lois shook her head. 'It was quite a task. George was reluctant to change anything. Any necessary repairs had to match the original.

Noah had another question. 'Why does the rear of the building look so different?'

This was a safe topic and Lois was happy to talk about anything to do with the house she loved. 'The north courtyard was meant to be a tennis court. It was all the rage in the seventeenth century, but Augustus died before the building was complete. His son was only interested in consolidating the family's standing and entertaining influential people. Then there was a fire, which destroyed the plans and the damage was repaired by people who did not really know what they were doing.' Lois shrugged. 'No one seems to have bothered with it since.' She remembered his first question. 'Oh, and the courtyard gets used by any tradesmen who need somewhere to put their things if there are repairs or decorations to do in the house.' She shook her head sadly. 'Not that anything has been done for a long time.'

Noah could understand that. Lois was doing a brilliant job in holding the estate together but saw herself as a mere caretaker and would not have initiated any major projects.

'What do you usually do on wet days?' Noah asked as they left the room.

'There are always letters to write and reports to go through. Things to arrange.'

'The managers seem competent.'

'Yes, but it all needs coordinating. To have someone to see the whole picture.'

It sounded a daunting task but she did not sound complaining. 'You must have some leisure time.'

'Of course. I enjoy reading. I have my embroidery and occasionally dabble in watercolour painting.' Lois gave a rueful smile. 'I am not very good.'

'I like drawing. I will show you my sketchbook sometime.'

Lois stopped so abruptly Noah almost bumped into her. 'The rest of the rooms can wait,' she said, changing their direction. 'We can start with the family portraits.'

That pleased Noah and he said, 'I don't have any family pictures apart from the sketches I have made myself.'

Lois led the way up the end staircase to the second floor and onto a long gallery. On one side, doors were interspersed by pictures. The opposite wall had large portraits between the un-curtained windows. Beneath them were tables and chests holding artifacts that might be worth looking at later.

They moved from one portrait to another with Lois naming the subjects and giving any interesting facts about their lives.

Noah was amazed by the familiarity of the men depicted. He could have been looking at himself, or as his grandfather might have looked in his youth. He was suddenly glad that his father had not resembled either of them.

'You are quite definitely a Laing,' Lois said, looking at him intently. Then she blushed and turned away.

'Was there any doubt?' he asked.

'Forgive me. The information we received from Australia was fragmented and has proved to be inaccurate. Ernest seems to have roamed far and wide. Anyone with an eye on advancement could have posed as his grandson.'

That was reasonable. He had needed to prove his identity to the Sydney lawyer before he was given any real information.

'I hesitated to mention it before, but, as you are intent on leaving anyway, I have to tell you that you do not automatically assume the title. As you were not born in this country the details will have to be verified.'

Noah shrugged his shoulders. 'Well, that is irrelevant given I don't want it.'

Lois moved on to the next portrait. 'This is George and his wife painted soon after their marriage. The are more, less formal, family pictures in other rooms.'

Noah had stopped listening as his eyes moved to the next portrait. It was smaller than the rest and in a much plainer frame.

'That is Ernest,' Lois said, but Noah had known it in a single glance. This was how he had always visualised Gramp in his youth. Without thinning hair and grey whiskers, the face was still instantly recognisable. His eyes held a hint of laughter, and he held his held at a familiar angle.

Lois watched the changing expressions on Noah's face. He was oblivious to her presence, lost in memories tender and sad. It was how she felt when she looked at the portrait of George that hung in her private parlour.

'Would I be allowed to take this home with me?' Noah asked quietly.

'It is yours.' Lois waved her arms in a wide circle as though encompassing the whole world. 'It is all yours. I only hold it in trust.' Even as she spoke, Lois knew she would fight tooth and nail to keep her own cherished picture.

The light was fading and Lois suggested they leave the rest of the pictures for another occasion. She crossed to the other side of the room and opened a door. 'This is the library but I don't think it is worth opening the shutters now. You can explore it at your leisure.'

Noah gave a last look at Ernest's portrait and, as he turned away, happened to glance through a window. He was surprised by the view and moved closer and looked down into an enclosed courtyard. The east and west wings extended back much further than he had realised and explained why he had been unable to find the archive room.

They retraced their steps to the head of the stairs and entered the east wing. Lois opened a wide door and said, 'This is the chapel,' and stepped inside.

Noah could not believe his eyes. It was like a miniature cathedral. Slender columns against the side walls arched up to meet overhead. Benches, enough to seat forty or more, were divided down the centre by a carpeted aisle. Ahead, behind the altar, was a large stained-glass window. The altar was draped in an embroidered cloth and held two large silver candlesticks. The light was dim but he could just see gilded plaques and pictures on the side walls.

Noah gave a low whistle.

Lois thought he was impressed until he said, 'Why did they go to so much trouble when there is a great church almost next door?'

It was not the reaction Lois had hoped for. 'There have been times in our history when Catholicism was frowned upon if not outright illegal,' she said coldly. 'The first baron's wife was of that religion. Although the Laings have been Church of England for several generations, and private services are still held here.'

Lois turned on her heel and went back to the landing. 'Perhaps you would be more interested in the games room downstairs.'

Noah closed the door quietly before he followed her down the stairs. 'I have already seen it,' he said when he drew level. 'I told you I did some exploring.' He raised an eyebrow and added,

'I assume I am permitted.' Lois stopped in her tracks, made to speak and thought better of it. She was not going to wrangle on the stairs and continued down to the drawing room. He had not seen a games room but her snooty manner annoyed him. He had never met such a prickly female and was tempted to let her stew. On second thought, he followed her into the room and closed the door.

She looked magnificent, a pint-sized warrior defending the Promised Land. Noah held up his hands in a gesture of surrender. 'Can we discuss this calmly? Please sit down and listen to my side of the story.'

Lois subsided onto the nearest sofa. She did not know what had come over her.

Noah did not sit. He did not think he would be welcome to share the sofa and was not going to start dragging furniture about. 'Lois, what you just said was unfair. You have no idea of my feelings. They do not matter at this moment. I will just repeat that I have commitments elsewhere and will not be staying permanently. I will however take advantage of my supposed ownership until I hear what to do next about Bill's problem.'

Lois hung her head for a second. 'I apologise. That remark was rude and uncalled for. You have been honest and I will be the same. I love this place but it is not mine. You are Baron Laing. You are here and I feel like a usurper every time I give an instruction.'

Noah moved closer and held out his hand. 'Truce?'

'Truce,' Lois replied, accepting the peace offering. 'I will just ask you not to spread your decision abroad. Laington is part of a larger community. What happens here affects everyone to some degree. I would be grateful if you could act as though you really are interested.'

'Agreed. I would be interested to see more. As you can guess, we have nothing like this at home.'

He saw her shoulders sag until she took a deep breath and raised her head. 'How long do you intend to stay?'

'I have no definite plans for the immediate future, but I will take advantage of my supposed position until I know what to do next.' That made him sound very shallow, as though he were cadging free board and lodging until he found something better to do. Lois deserved better.

'You will remember that Bill wants to locate any of his family still living. I will leave him to tell you as much of his history as he is prepared to share but we think he has a brother and are awaiting news of his whereabouts.'

'Oh, I am so glad.' Lois smiled. 'I like Bill and hope he finds a happy ending.'

There did not seem to be anything else to say so Lois excused herself and fled to the privacy of her rooms.

Lois went straight to her parlour and stood in front of George's portrait. 'What am I going to do?' she whispered. The beloved face gazed back at her with a benign smile, and she felt instantly comforted. George had been the rock on which her life was built from the day he had come to rescue her and her mama. He had never been too busy to listen and advise. She missed him so much.

George could not advise her now but she felt his presence like a warm embrace. His voice seemed to echo in her mind. *Now, now. There is no problem that cannot be solved by patience and careful thought.* Lois smiled and blew a kiss to the picture. As she turned away, the beloved voice cautioned, *But we do not always get what we want.'*

What Lois wanted was for Noah to love Laington enough to stay.

Chapter 8

Bill joined Lois and Noah for dinner. He had been exploring on his own. 'I went upstairs,' he admitted, looking at Lois to see whether he had been trespassing. Reassured, he launched into a recital of what he had discovered.

'There are all sorts of things up there. Piles of furniture and a room where a girl was sewing. And a room full of toys!' Bill's rugged face was alight with childish wonder. 'I never had toys,' Bill admitted sadly. 'Sometimes we made a bundle to kick about but not much else. I saw things in the shop windows and wished I could get them for Lucy.'

The food grew cold on their plates. Now he had started to talk, Bill could not stop. Years of worry and keeping out of trouble had supressed his natural zest for life.

Noah and Lois listened, enthralled, as Bill told them about his youth. It had been hard but there had been some security in a loving family unit. Until his father was killed in an accident. From then on it had been left to Mrs Norton and ten-year-old Bill to scrape a living, doing whatever work they could. His little sister, Lucy, was constantly ill with what sounded very much like consumption. One day, while working at the docks, Bill had pocketed an orange that had fallen from a damaged crate, thinking it would be a treat for Lucy. Other dockers were doing the same but only Bill had been caught and charged with theft. He might have got off with a lesser sentence than transportation, but he had lost his temper in the dock and harangued the judge with a lecture on the unfairness of his arrest and society in general.

Bill paused, eyes lowered, as he remembered the past. Pulling himself together, he looked at his companions with a rueful smile. 'After that I learned to keep my mouth shut.'

'I am very touched and grateful that you have opened up now,' Lois said sadly. 'Life is unfair. We don't always get what we expect. I think you are a very brave man and I hope you find your brother.'

'I have only told Lois that we are waiting for news. I would not have told her anything else, even if I had known.' Noah was torn between reassuring Bill and wondering what had been behind Lois's statement. He recalled her mentioning that her father had been a gambler and suspected her life had not been all privilege and comfort.

Lois rang the small bell beside her plate, glad that she had dismissed the staff from the room. A footman came to clear the plates and Pound supervised the serving of the dessert course.

When Bill was suitably refuelled with two helpings of apple pie and cream, a large slice of cake and topped up with cheese and wafers, he sat back with a contented sigh. Noah topped up his friend's glass with the beer he preferred to wine.

Lois smiled and dared to asked if he would tell her a little more about his family.

Bill's expression clouded. He took a long pull at his drink before telling her that his mum and little Lucy had died in the workhouse. 'That was before I had even left England, but nobody told me. I spent years worrying about them when they were already safe in the arms of Jesus.'

The simple statement of faith brought tears to Lois's eyes and told her where he had found the strength to survive. She was not overly religious. She attended church and found solace in the wonders of nature but had largely given up prayers that did not receive satisfactory answers.

Noah reached across and gently squeezed her hand. He had been with Bill when they were told of the deaths. Bill had borne the news stoney-faced and only shown his emotion by kicking the workhouse gatepost when they left.

Bill leant forward. 'My brother Fred was only twelve and ran away.' He looked gratefully at Noah. 'But Noah went all over the place trying to find him. Well,' Bill qualified, 'not really. He visited people I would never have thought of and dipped into his pocket time and again.'

With Noah filling in the details, Lois learned how they had spent their time in London. Not rollicking but going through official channels to discover that Fred had joined the navy. Lois could imagine the lad, if he was anything like Bill, preparing himself for a voyage to Australia in search of his brother.

'Now Fred is away on a ship somewhere but Noah has arranged to be told when he returns.'

So they would be here for an indefinite period, Lois thought with relief. Perhaps a deeper knowledge of his inheritance would persuade Noah to stay.

That night she slept peacefully, although the future still hung in the balance.

The rain had stopped by morning but the sky was overcast, and Lois wrapped up warmly for her visit to the market. She sat between Noah and Farmer on the front seat of a wagon. It had just enough room for them not to be squashed but meant that their shoulders touched from time to time. Lois appeared oblivious of the intimacy but Noah was quite enjoying it. It had been a long time since he had been close to a soft, feminine body.

The town centre was all bustle and noise. Farmer left them outside the church and went to fill the list of supplies given to him by the cook and housekeeper.

'Where first?' Noah asked, stepping to her side to shield her from the water being splashed up by a passing wagon. Lois acknowledged the courtesy with a smile.

'Mrs Laing!' called a middle-aged woman who was selling eggs from a straw-lined basket. 'Our Jeanie had a little girl last night. I would have sent you word but guessed you would be here this morning.'

'Thank you, Mrs Butler. I will arrange for a birthing gift if I cannot manage to visit myself.'

'I expect you have been busy showing Baron Laing around.' It was an obvious request for an introduction, and Lois complied. 'Is it a grandchild?' Noah asked and, at Mrs Butler's energetic nod, he added, 'Congratulations.'

Lois nudged him away from the stall and when they were out of earshot, she commented, 'I think that is the seventh or eighth. But each and every one is welcome with open arms. Mr Butler will be wetting the baby's head, as they say. Enough to drown the mite!'

Numerous other greetings and snippets of news were given as they continued their progress. Lois was obviously well-liked and respected. Noah came in fair few greetings himself, many of which consisted of congratulations or a subtle question. He dealt with them all in the same quiet, non-committal manner that gave nothing of his thoughts away. More direct questions came from the better-dressed people strolling between the stalls. He neither confirmed nor denied pleasure in his inheritance. Even the wizened old lady who stared up from under the brim of her bonnet and loudly directed him to marry Lois and give her a child at last did not shake his composure. Bystanders were grinning and Lois wished she was equally un-embarrassed.

'Well done,' she congratulated him when they came to an unoccupied space. Noah just grinned. 'Mrs Whittaker can be embarrassingly outspoken.'

They completed their circuit of the market and eventually re-joined Farmer for the drive back to the manor.

'That was an interesting outing,' Noah said once they were indoors. 'Will it be the same at church tomorrow?'

'I am afraid so,' Lois said, pleased that he had decided to join them. 'I told you Laington is part of the community. What happens here affects everyone to some degree.'

And so it was next day. Lois delayed their arrival at the church until after the bells had rung and they could make their way to a pew at the front of the church unmolested. On the way out, Noah was displayed and assessed like a prize ram.

Lois introduced him to Lady Hamilton-Klein. 'I am so pleased to meet you, Lord Laing,' the seductive brunette murmured in a husky voice and squeezed Noah's fingers as they shook hands. Noah guessed she was older than she wished to appear. She was firmly corseted in a way that elevated her voluptuous breasts and her dark eyes held an open invitation. 'My husband has recently returned from a mission to the colony. Did you, perhaps, travel on the same ship?'

Noah withdrew his hand and replied calmly, 'Most unlikely. I came by cattle boat and did not mix with the other passengers.'

Lady Hamilton-Klein ignored the rebuff with a throat laugh. 'How droll. You must come and tell me all about it. My husband is still in London, giving his report to the prime minister, you know.'

Noah admitted that he did not know. 'I spent very little time in London. Please excuse me, we are blocking the door.'

Lois was secretly chuckling to herself. He did not like Vera HK! There were rumours that she had not been lonely during her husband's year-long absence and frequently entertained, young men being in the majority. There was no opportunity to comment as there were more people waiting to be introduced.

Among them was a tall, quietly spoken man who Lois introduced as Mr Collins, the local school master. 'I hope you will continue to allow us to use your library, my lord. It is such a valuable resource for children who know little of the world beyond our parish boundaries.' Noah remembered Lois saying something about a school at the manor had a horrified vision of children pulling books from the shelves. He cast a quick look at Lois. She gave a slight nod and Noah found enough voice to reassure the school master before the next person edged forward for an introduction.

In the carriage, on the way back to the manor, Noah asked why children were using the library.

'There was a fire that destroyed much of the school. I have been allowing Mr Collins to use one of the rooms in the north wing. He collects books for his lessons and returns them afterwards.'

Hattie, who had travelled with them, added that she taught the girls sewing while Mr Collins was absent. She also had plenty to say about Mrs Hamilton-Klein. 'I don't know how she dares to look down her nose at me! She could not have made her invitation plainer if it was painted on a banner.'

'There's no need to advertise if the goods are worth having.' Bill smiled across the carriage at Hattie. 'There's a difference between brass and gold.'

'Well, she has enough brass for a set of church bells!' Hattie snorted.

Noah was enjoying the double-entendres. 'I would go for the gold that has been tried and tested for quality,' he advised helpfully, and he received a sharp nudge in the ribs from Bill. He was also enjoying Lois's pretence that she did not know what was going on.

Chapter 9

The days fell into a pattern. Without discussion, the men had formed a habit of joining Lois for breakfast at seven thirty where they arranged the day's activities. Bill had offered his help to the head shepherd and often did not return to the manor at night. Lambing was in full swing and he proved to have a gift for dealing with difficult births.

Lois gently eased Noah into the role of baron in the hope it would persuade him to stay. Noah played his part to perfection. As long as they avoided touchy subjects, they were enjoying each other's company.

Noah attended the managers' meetings and learned that the estate extended beyond the manor, grounds and local farms. There was a quarry several miles to the west and two woollen mills in another town. His respect for Lois grew. She carried the responsibilities with a quiet assurance that defied challenge without being overbearing. At the meetings, Lois consulted Noah for his opinion before a decision was made. It all seemed so natural, the process of a new baron gradually finding his feet.

They visited some of the people he had met at church, and Lois encouraged him to accept invitations that did not include her. One such invitation was from John Partridge to join a men-only cards evening. Lois thought she had concealed her disquiet until Noah mentioned it when they were alone.

'There is no need for you to be worried. I play cards but I am not a gambler.' He was a competent player and it was a pleasant way to spend an evening, but not something he would want to do on a regular basis.

'Sorry. I hope John did not notice.'

'You do realise that he has hopes in your direction?'

'I do not plan to remarry.'

Noah changed the subject and Lois relaxed.

She hoped he was coming around to the idea of staying. But she dared not ask. It was not her way to rock a steady boat.

The informal reception Lois had mentioned was converted into an open day. The degree of interest Noah had aroused made an evening event unmanageable. There would either have been too many people vying for his attention or many who would feel slighted at not receiving an invitation.

At breakfast on the proposed open day, Lois told the men what to expect. Bill groaned and disappeared as soon as he had finished eating. Noah did not have that freedom.

Midmorning, Noah joined Lois on the front steps to accept respectful congratulations and greeting from the lesser folk, mostly workers and the just plain curious. He thanked them with equal courtesy and said refreshments were available in the servants' hall.

He had already met some of the later arrivals. The business owners and professional men accompanied by their wives. These visitors were allowed into the house and what Noah thought of as the managers' drawing room. He circulated among them as they helped themselves from a general buffet laid out on the long table.

There was a lull during which Noah and Lois enjoyed their own lunch.

At two o'clock a line of carriages started to make their way up the drive. Pound admitted these visitors and announced them at the main drawing room door. Maids carried around trays of wine and dainty snacks as Noah went through the courtesies again.

Noah found it the least enjoyable part of the day. People had come from further afield. There were several sirs and their ladies, a retired brigadier, the gentry and prominent businessmen including the local member of parliament. Their curiosity was more open, and Noah had to field difficult questions about his future plans.

One visitor he could well have done without was Mrs Hamilton-Klein. She latched on to Noah's arm and tried to take over the introductions. His attempt to move away only made the woman rub her breast against his arm.

Mrs Hamilton-Klein was ousted by Mrs Whittaker. 'Stop behaving like a huzzy, Vera. Laing is quite capable of standing without your support!' The loud statement was accompanied by a thump of her cane perilously close to Mrs Hamilton-Klein's foot.

Mrs Hamilton-Klein gave a haughty shake of her head and stalked away, and she was followed by the equally loud remark, 'She never could resist anything in trousers.'

There was a rise in the level of background conversations as everyone tried to fill the uncomfortable silence. Mrs Whittaker eyed Noah from head to foot. Her eyes where sparkling when she leant forward to whisper, 'You look just like George. If I were fifty years younger, I might have another go myself.' She moved away with a naughty chuckle.

It was late afternoon before the last visitors left.

Noah poured himself a brandy and a sherry for Lois before flopping onto one of the settees in the drawing room. He loosened his collar and gave a sigh of relief.

'Thank God that is over. I hope never to experience such a fiasco again.'

Lois was in a buoyant mood. She thought the day had gone exceptionally well. 'I cannot guarantee there will not be an incident but the open day is a tradition at New Year and the baron's birthday.'

'Well, that need not bother me. I will be long gone.'

Lois's bubble of happiness burst, and she spoke without thinking. 'I don't know why you bothered to come at all. It certainly took you long enough.'

Noah sat up and faced her. His frayed nerves overrode caution and his voice was harsh. 'I told you I had commitments. I was concerned and came as soon as I could.'

'So concerned that it took you five years! George couldn't wait any longer and died in mental and physical agony!'

'Don't exaggerate. It is not even two.'

They both realised their voices had risen and stopped dead. They were quarrelling loud enough for the staff to hear. Lois slammed her glass down on a side table and ran out of the room.

Noah started to follow her but thought better of it. Her last words rang in his ears. Had there been earlier letters that had gone astray? Had the old man been sick and in pain for so long? At least his beloved Gramp had not died in agony.

Feeling as weary as an old man, Noah climbed the stairs to his room.

Lois threw herself onto her bed and wept tears of pain, anger and shame.

What had come over her? This was the second time she had stormed away from Noah. She never lost her temper. She had once seen her mother in a rage, throwing crockery at a closed door and screaming. It was ugly and frightening, and Lois never wanted to be like that.

Now she had opened the door to questions she had avoided answering. She now knew Noah well enough to know that he would not leave matters here.

Lois heard Sarah moving about in the dressing room and sat up. Dinner had been rearranged to a later time than usual to allow for a rest period after the visitors had left. Lois didn't have an appetite but she was not a coward and would not hide in her room. She sighed and went through to the dressing room.

Sarah took one look at her mistress's face and went down to the kitchen for some ice. Lois had undressed and washed by the time she returned.

Lois sat at the dressing table staring at her red eyes and blotchy skin, and her resolve not to hide weakened. Sarah's reflection appeared over her shoulder and she offered a white pad. 'Ice,' Sarah said and started to unpin Lois's hair. Lois held the compress over her eyes for as long as she could bear the stinging cold.

Sarah helped her to finish dressing and held out the powder pot. 'Just a light dusting,' she suggested.

The dinner gong sounded and Lois squared her shoulder and took a deep breath. Halfway to the door she turned and came back to give Sarah a quick hug and whisper, 'Thank you.'

Noah waited for the dinner gong before he left his room. As he closed the bedroom door, Bill stepped onto the landing, blocking his view of Lois, who was leaving her room.

Noah paused but the sound of swishing skirts told him Lois was approaching, and he forced his feet to move.

Bill took a step back to allow Lois and Noah to meet at the head of the stairs. One glance at their faces warned him to keep quiet. He was adept at gauging moods. It helped to stay out of trouble if you knew how others were feeling.

Noah automatically offered his arm and, after the briefest hesitation, Lois accepted his support down the stairs. Noah clenched his muscles slightly to keep her hand in place until they reached the small dining doom. They took their places at the table and Lois signalled for the soup to be served.

The only words spoken during the meal were to the staff.

'I'm going to see Hattie,' Bill blurted out as soon as he had finished his dessert. The footman had to jump out of the way as Bill dashed for the door.

Lois and Noah stood more slowly. 'May we go to the drawing room?' Noah asked quietly. Lois nodded and moved ahead of him.

With the drawing room door safely closed, they subsided into their usual chairs.

'I apologise,' Noah and Lois began, and Noah added, 'Please listen to me first.'

Lois sat with lowered eyes as Noah began. 'We need to clear the air about those letters. I have only received one and that was in August '72.' He was never likely to forget that date. 'I could not leave then or for the next several months. Perhaps I should have written but I had other things on my mind. I can only add that I am sorry for your distress.'

Lois sighed. 'I am sorry too. I don't know why I...' She looked up at him. 'Yes, I do. I thought the day had gone so well. We are accustomed to Mrs Whittaker's outspokenness. She is liked and tolerated. As for Vera' – Lois shrugged – 'I don't think it is gossiping to say what you probably guess. Vera has a reputation for, let us say, not being lonely when her husband is away.'

'There is more to it than that,' Noah prompted.

'Yes. I was in such a good mood and you reminded me about leaving. I came down off my cloud with a bump and spoke from disappointment.'

Noah knew that was not all, but Lois looked so downcast he could not press her further right now. But he still had questions.

'Please excuse me,' Lois said, getting to her feet. 'I feel so tired. Perhaps we will both feel more in harmony after a good night's sleep.'

Noah watched her go, doubting either of them would sleep well. He paced the room. He could not get her earlier statement out of his mind. He knew how hard it was to watch a loved one die. At least Gramp had not been in pain.

How long had she been carrying all the responsibility? He had never got round to checking the date of George's death, but it had to be within the last two years. Tomorrow, he would show her the letter he had received and try to explain why he had not come immediately.

Chapter 10

Noah's summons to Plymouth arrived with the next morning's post. He was given no time to talk to Lois privately as Bill was as excited as a child at Christmas and could not wait to leave. Their farewells were frustratingly brief and Noah's assurance of a swift return left Lois torn between relief and apprehension.

There was no direct train to Plymouth and the men had to change trains twice with long delays between connections. Bill kept asking when they would get there, part excited and part anxious that Fred would not be pleased to see an ex-convict. Noah sympathised but it was wearing on the nerves. On top of that the weather had turned cold and rainy.

By the time they reached Plymouth it was close to midnight.

Weary in mind and body, Noah told the cab driver to take them to a hotel. Any would do for tonight.

The hotel they were taken to turned out to be little more than a boarding house. A sleepy youth showed them to rooms, basic but clean, and Noah asked about a meal.

'Dinner's finished. There's a tavern down the road a bit,' the boy offered dubiously, glancing out of the window at the pouring rain.

'I'm starving,' Bill complained.

'I might be able to find something in the kitchen if you are not too fussy.'

Noah was past caring. The sooner Bill was fed and bedded the better he would like it.

They followed the lad down to a room with a long, scrubbed table and benches. It was a far cry from the opulence of their recent surrounds. After much muttering and clanging from the kitchen, they boy gave them some cold pie and tankards of ale.

It was nearly 2 a.m. before Noah climbed into his narrow bed.

The late night did not affect Bill. He was knocking on Noah's door while it was still dark outside.

'Sit down and be quiet!' Noah ordered grumpily. 'It is too early to go to the dockyard. Wait while I get dressed and we will try to get some breakfast.'

The proprietor was a fat middle-aged woman, over-awed at having a titled gentleman as a guest. She apologised profusely, saying, 'I'm sure this is not what your lordship is used to.'

Noah smiled and said he had slept in much worse places and asked about breakfast.

The were joined at the table by three men in rough working clothes. Their casual enquiry into the reason for Noah and Bill's visit set Bill off into a recital of their search for his brother.

'Don't get there too early,' one of the workmen advised. 'The bigwigs don't start as early as us.'

Despite the warning, Bill was impatient and badgered Noah so much he gave in and they set off for the docks. It had stopped raining but a strong, salt-laden wind reminded Noah unpleasantly of his arrival in England. Hopefully, the coming interview would not hold as many shocks.

Noah showed his letter of introduction to the gate sentry and they were directed to the main building. The uniformed clerk read the letter and told them to wait in the hall. The bench was hard and the hall draughty as men came and went. Noah was hard put to keep Bill from accosting them to ask if they knew his brother.

Eventually, they were called into an office and the letter was read again. 'Wait here,' the man at the desk said and took the letter through to another room.

A few moments later, a captain came out to meet them.

'Lord Laing? Please come through to my office and take a seat.' When Bill made to follow, the captain frowned. 'Your man can wait here.'

'This is Mr Norton, brother of the man we are seeking,' Noah replied.

The captain gave Bill a disdainful stare and said, 'Oh, a rating I assume,' and ushered Noah into his office. Noah took the chair in front of the desk, but Bill was not offered a seat.

The captain sat behind his desk and said, with mock sorrow, 'This does make matters difficult, my lord. I only have the names of the officers.'

Noah raised an eyebrow and stayed silent. He was not going to be fobbed off so easily. The captain gave a nervous cough followed by a brief smile. 'The best I can do is give you a pass to speak to the captain of the Camptown.' He rang a small bell on his desk and the underling appeared so quickly Noah though he must have been listening at the door. The captain handed over Noah's letter and gave a command and stood. 'My clerk will attend to you. Good day.'

Noah took his time in rising. He held out his hand until the captain was forced to stand and shake it. 'Thank you for your help,' Noah said blandly and followed the clerk from the room. The pass was written and handed to Noah, along with his letter and a smile. 'Good luck, sir,' the man whispered with a cautious glance at the connecting door.

Bill managed to remain silent until they were out of the building. 'Uppity sod,' he muttered. 'As though ordinary sailors don't matter. Who does he think does all the bloody work?'

'I am glad you did not give vent to those feelings in there,' Noah replied. 'I know it is hard but we won't get anywhere if we put people's backs up.'

The pass got them through to the dock where the Camptown was berthed. They were just in time to see a senior officer step off the gangplank. Noah stepped into his path and enquired, 'Captain Blake? I have been given a pass' – Noah held it out – 'to speak to you about Fred Norton.'

'Is he in trouble?'

'No, sir. He is the brother of Mr Norton here.' Noah indicated Bill. ''They lost touch with each other and he hopes they can be reunited.'

'Then I am sorry I cannot help you. Norton left the ship in the Caribbean. He had served longer than he'd signed on for and was free to resign. A good man. I was sorry to lose him.'

Bill groaned. 'Don't you know where he went?'

The captain was sympathetic and shook his head. 'Go aboard and speak to my first officer. Maybe one of the men will know where Norton went. Please excuse me. I must go to make my report.' Noah thanked him and they shook hands.

The captain yelled up to the deck and pointed at Noah before hurrying on his way, saying good luck to Bill as he passed.

Noah and Bill were met at the top of the gangplank by a harassed-looking man ticking items off a long list. Noah repeated his story and several seamen were called down to speak to him briefly. Bill was almost hopping with excitement.

The men were willing to talk but could not be released immediately and arrangements were made for a meeting late that afternoon. The way Noah jingled the coins in his pocket ensured the appointment would be kept.

It was progress at last.

There was no point in hanging around the dockyard for hours and Noah managed to drag Bill away. 'What are we going to do?' Bill wailed.

'We wait with as much patience as we can,' Noah told him, his own patience wearing thin. 'I am going to write a letter. You can read or sleep.' To ensure a few hours of peace and quiet, Noah bought a newspaper to keep Bill occupied.

Noah had not thought to bring his writing case. It was one of his few treasured possessions and held all his Identity documents was well as fond memories. In any case, he had not expected to be away long enough to need it. But he now needed to let Lois know they had been delayed.

Noah begged paper and a pen from the boarding house lady and retired to his room. There was no desk, so Noah moved the bowl from the washstand and settled down to write to Lois.

How should he start? 'Dear Lois' seemed too personal. They had reached an uneasy truce but were hardly on affectionate terms. 'Dear Mrs Laing' sounded too formal. He dipped the pen and started to write the date. Ink splattered from the bent nib and Noah swore under his breath. Why did everything have to be so annoying?

Noah rummaged in his valise and found a pencil. He turned the paper over and started again.

Trying to think what to say, Noah began to doodle. Images of Lois, smiling or cross, wearing her fluffy knitted hat or with her hair piled high on her head soon filled the page. Noah stared at them in surprise. Had he watched her so closely that he could capture her image from memory? He had to admit she was worth staring at. She tried to hide her feelings behind a polite mask but her thoughts were reflected in her eyes, no matter how hard she tried to appear impassive.

Noah started to screw up the paper. He was getting too involved. The room did not contain a waste bin and Noah was loathe to throw the drawings in the empty fire-grate. He smoothed the paper out again, folded it and put it in his pocket.

Noah lay on the bed for want of any easy chair and stared at the dingy ceiling. The paper in his pocket crackled as he moved and he gave a huff of frustration. Even on paper the woman attracted his attention. He knew it was not intentional. When she was not being an instructor, Lois kept her distance. Even when they were apparently at ease there was an invisible barrier between them. Noah knew that was partly his fault. It was not in his nature to form false relationships. There could be no mutual future for them. Lois was wedded to the estate. He gave a cynical laugh. That was one way of putting it. She had firmly stated that she had no intention of marrying again. Neither did he! He would soon be gone. Time and distance would wipe her from his mind.

Sleep temporarily had that effect as he dozed.

A heavy knock on his door woke Noah from his nap. Bill entered, anxious to get to their meeting in plenty of time. 'I don't want to miss them,' he said as he nagged Noah to hurry.

No specific time had been mentioned but 'late afternoon' suggested after five rather than before. Noah delayed for as long as he could stand Bill's fidgeting but refused to hang around the dock gates. He found a window seat in a nearby tavern and dampened Bill's anxiety with food. It was close to seven o'clock when a stream of seamen exited the dockyard gates.

Bill rushed to meet them, his words tumbling over themselves as he began to ask about Fred. Noah managed to separate their informants from their curios comrades and suggested he wait until they could find somewhere reasonably private to talk. 'Easier to talk once we've wet our whistles,' the younger man added expectantly.

The hint was no more than Noah had expected. Information had to be paid for.

Once they were settled in a quiet corner of a tavern further away from the docks, Noah waited until the first round had been drunk before he allowed Bill to talk.

'Do you know where Fred went?'

Ben, the older man, shook his head. 'Not exactly. He just said he had got taken on as second mate on a cargo ship.'

'He was always a cut above us,' the younger man added. He looked sideways at Bill. 'You the convict he wanted to find?'

Ben elbowed him in the ribs and told him to get another round in. Noah obligingly dropped some coins onto the table.

'Sorry about that,' Ben said. 'Fred made it no secret that his brother had been unfairly convicted. He took the chance of transferring to a merchant ship in the hope of finding a way to Australia to find him.'

'Do you know the name of the ship?' Noah asked as Mac, the younger man, returned with the tankards. 'Some sort of bird. Can't remember the name.'

Bill groaned and Noah shook his head. More coins were laid on the table. 'Is there anything you can remember?'

Mac had his nose in the tankard, leaving his mate to answer.

'Well, it was going to Bristol with a cargo of sugar.'

'Where were you? The Caribbean has a lot of islands.'

'Jamaica.'

It was a start but the men did not have anything else of value to tell them. Noah rose and thanked them, leaving a shiny gift on the table, and dragged Bill from the tavern.

'It's hopeless,' Bill said morosely. 'There must be all sorts of ships taking sugar to England. How will we find one we don't even know the name of?'

'Buck up. We go to Bristol and ask questions.'

It was an easier journey next day as there was a direct rail link between the two ports. Noah had intended to send a telegram to Lois, to say they had been delayed, but their train was ready to leave. He would contact her from Bristol.

Noah's first task on arrival was to book into a decent hotel. The boarding house had been adequate for a couple of nights but heaven only knew how long it would take them to find a bird-named ship from Jamaica!

For several days they went from one shipping company to another. Noah thought he could recite details of their mission in his sleep, they were repeated so many times. He had not realised how many companies used the port. He found that presenting one of the cards Lois had had printed for him at least got them a polite reception. An accompanying coin even gained a few suggestions of where to search next.

He was on the point of admitting defeat when they had a breakthrough. The desk clerk at Drayton Shipping said they had a ship called the *Heron*. It did carry sugar but had just arrived from Barbados. He was kind enough to look through his ledger and gave an exclamation of triumph.

'There we have it! *Heron* called at several islands, including Jamaica. Barbados was the last.' He beamed at Noah and Bill. 'It docked several days ago, was unloaded and sent to a working yard for some repairs!' He gave them the name of the yard. Noah thanked him and the clerk pocketed his reward with a smile. Bill shook his hand, too overcome with gratitude for words.

Just as they were leaving, the clerk called Noah back and spoke quietly. 'I don't have the names of the crew but Captain McCoy is staying at the Crown Hotel. Good luck.'

Bill wanted to go straight to the yard but Noah stalled for time. He did not want to disappoint Bill too soon. If the ship had been unloaded and sent for repairs, there was a chance the crew had been dismissed and Fred had already left to search for a ship that would take him to Australia.

'I need to find a bank before they close for the day.'

Bill stopped. 'I'll never be able to repay you. I've lost count of how many palms you've greased.'

'So have I,' Noah replied cheerfully. 'My grandfather always said money was only good for the good it could do. If – no, *when* – we find Fred, we will call it money well spent.'

Or money down the drain, Noah thought to himself.

Noah had a plan. He would do the next stage of the search alone. Bill could be intimidating or overtalkative and what Noah had in mind required finesse. They went to the hotel and Noah collected a single bag. 'Stay here. I hope I won't be too long.'

Noah walked into the Crown Hotel and approached the desk. Another of his cards was placed face up on the counter. 'Have you a room? My friend, Captain McCoy, recommended you.'

The bait was taken. 'Captain McCoy is staying with us now. I believe he is in the smoking room.'

Noah said thank you and asked to leave his bag while he greeted his old friend.

There was only one person in the smoking room, hidden behind a newspaper and a cloud of smoke. A rather battered cap lying on the table beside him confirmed a naval connection.

Noah paused by his chair. 'Captain McCoy?' he asked politely.

The paper was lowered to reveal the face of a man well past middle age. It was tanned and surrounded by a hedge of greying whiskers, from which protruded a clay pipe.

'You do not know me, sir, but I am on an errand of mercy for a friend. Please will you spare me a few moments?'

Captain McCoy was intrigued. He had spent a boring week kicking his heels while he waited to reclaim his ship. He could do with some entertainment. He invited Noah to sit and laid aside his pipe.

'Now, young man, what is this about?'

Noah recited his tale until the captain started to laugh. 'That is as good a yarn as I have heard in an age. Friend! It's your brother!'

Noah started to deny it, but the captain was still speaking. 'Your accent gave you away. As soon as you mentioned Australia and Fred Norton I knew who you were.' He frowned and stared for a moment. 'Not that you look anything like him.'

Noah handed over one of his cards, which the captain read before chuckling again. 'Either you have gone to a lot of trouble to conceal your background or you really are Baron Noah Laing. But I will hear you out.'

Captain McCoy invited Noah to sit and called for a jug of punch. Then he relit his pipe and settled back to listen.

'Norton is a good man,' McCoy said when Noah had finished. 'He was straight with me when I took him on. I don't judge men by the actions of others. He had a good record from the navy, a reference from his captain and an ugly face that showed every emotion. Meet me at the shipyard tomorrow at ten. Now it is time for my dinner. Will you join me?'

Noah thanked him. 'I would be honoured but Bill will be chewing the furniture waiting for me to return. Thank you for your help. I will see you tomorrow.'

Noah retrieved his bag and said he would not be needing a room after all.

Noah had barely stepped out of the hotel before Bill rushed up, demanding, 'What did he say? Does he know where Fred has gone?'

Noah steered him away from the entrance and started walking. 'You can meet Fred tomorrow.'

Bill took him in a bear hug and whirled in a circle, letting out a wordless shout of joy. Crashing into a wall was the only thing that stopped them landing in a heap on the ground. 'Drunk!' tutted a lady passing by.

The blast of beery breath told Noah where Bill had been waiting. He wriggled free and dragged his exuberant companion into a side street. 'For God's sake, shut up! Do you want to get arrested?'

When they reached the hotel, Bill called out to the desk clerk, 'I am going to see Freddie tomorrow.' The clerk looked shocked and retreated to a room behind the desk.

With a great effort, Noah managed to get Bill up the stairs and along the corridor to his room. 'The key,' Noah hissed as Bill jiggled the door handle. 'Where is your blasted key?'

'I'm going to see Fred tomorrow,' Bill told him with a broad smile. 'He's my brother.'

Noah had to wedge Bill against the door frame to rummage in his pockets for the key. He unlocked the door and Bill's weight swung it open. He took two or three steps and landed face down on the bed. Noah looked at him, torn between amusement and annoyance.

'I am not putting you to bed,' Noah said as he hauled off Bill's boots. 'Don't complain about a sore head in the morning.' As he closed the door, he wondered if Bill would sleep until morning. The last thing he wanted was for Bill to wake in the early hours and start hammering on his door wanting to know when he could meet Fred. He thought Bill would sleep for at least a couple of hours, so he locked the door and went down to the dining room.

After his meal, Noah asked for a pot of strong coffee to be sent up to Bill's room. As he crossed the hallway, he was waylaid by the frowning hotel manager. 'Lord Laing, this is a respectable hotel for gentlemen. If you cannot control your servant, I will have to ask you to leave.'

Noah apologised for the disturbance, not bothering to explain that Bill was not a servant. He was certainly not a gentleman! Noah could feel a disapproving glare burning into his back as he climbed the stairs.

Bill was still sprawled across the bed, snoring into the pillow. Noah did not try to rouse him until the coffee arrived.

It was no easy task getting Bill's limp body propped up against the headboard, and Noah was out of breath by the time he was sure Bill would not just slide off the other side of the bed. 'Get this down you,' Noah growled, holding the cup to Bill's mouth. Bill took a swig and jerked upright, spilling coffee over Noah's sleeve. 'What? Where am I?'

'At least you are awake,' Noah said, dabbing his wet sleeve with a towel. 'Drink that coffee without spitting it back up. I am not talking to you until you do.' He sat with folded arms and a stern frown until Bill did as he was told.

Whether it was the coffee or the threat of not hearing about Fred that sobered Bill, he drank the coffee, and Noah poured a second cup, shuddering with distaste.

'Will you tell me now?' he asked meekly.

Noah could not stay annoyed with his friend and put him out of his misery. 'We were within a few yards of Fred at the shipyard. He had been left as caretaker when the rest of the crew came ashore. We are going to meet him at ten o'clock tomorrow.'

'Can't we—'

'No! We cannot go any earlier. Now get some proper sleep. I will see you tomorrow.' Noah had reached the door and turned back. 'Stay here until I come. I don't want you knocking on my door asking if it is time to go.' Noah managed not to laugh until he was safely in his own room.

As he undressed, the drawing in his pocket crackled, reminding him yet again of Lois. He really ought to write to let her know why they had been delayed. He had tried several times but could not find the right words. He could not say he was missing her even if it was true. A plain statement of facts would have sounded as though he was still resentful about their argument. The longer he put off writing, the more confused he became.

Chapter 11

Noah and Bill reached the dock gates a few minutes before ten. Punctual to the dot, Captain McCoy walked towards them and shook hands with Noah. He turned to Bill. 'Well, there is no doubt you are Fred Norton's brother. Follow me.'

The gate sentry saluted the captain and asked Noah and Bill to sign in as visitors.

Fred had not been warned of the coming reunion and when he came on deck to greet his captain, he stopped as though he had walked into an invisible wall. His eyes opened wide and his mouth formed the word, 'Bill?' but no sound emerged.

Bill took a step forward. 'Freddie?' Within seconds the two men were in each other's arms, unashamedly crying. Noah felt a lump in his throat and turned his head just in time to see McCoy wiping his own eyes. 'That's a job well done,' the captain said gruffly. Raising his voice, he called, 'Norton! Is this the way to greet your captain on board?'

The brothers sprang apart but before either could speak, the captain was clapping them both on the shoulder. 'You have both got your wish. Now fetch your things and be on your way.'

Fred came to attention. 'No, sir! You have been good to me. I will not leave you in the lurch.'

'Perkins will be here within the hour. Now get your things. That is an order!'

Although the words were rough, McCoy's whiskery face was smiling. 'Good luck to you both.' He turned to Noah. 'I hope they get around to thanking you, Lord Laing,' he said, chuckling, 'once they come down to earth again.'

Noah watched him disappear into the depths of the ship and walked over to the brothers. He held out his hand to Fred. 'Bill has forgotten to introduce me. I am Noah Laing and I am very pleased to meet you at last.'

'He's a lord!' Bill added. 'A good one. You should know all—'

'Leave that for now, Bill,' Noah told him. 'The sooner Fred completes his duties, the sooner we can be on our way.' To Fred he added, 'I will take him out of your way now. We are staying at the Brown Goose Hotel on Lester Road. I will book you a room and you can join us there as soon as you are free.'

'Thank you, sir, your lordship.'

'I'm staying here!' The brothers spoke together then Fred gave Bill a shove. 'Go now, and don't worry. I'll join you as soon as I can.'

Bill left the ship and yard reluctantly but refused to return to the hotel. 'I'm staying here.'

Noah shrugged his shoulders. 'Stay if you must but don't, and I repeat don't, you dare go to a tavern. We were nearly evicted last night!'

'I've learned my lesson,' Bill replied humbly. 'I won't let you down again.'

Noah hoped Bill could stick to that resolve. It would take courage for a man of Bill's size and appearance to refuse a drink.

The hotel clerk looked amazed when Noah tried to book a room for another Mr Norton. 'I will have to ask if we have one free,' he stammered before going to knock on the door to the back room. The manager came to the desk.

'Lord Laing...'

Noah held up a hand for silence. 'If you do not have a room for my guest, we will find another hotel. All three of us. Last night was an aberration. Mr Bill Norton had just discovered the whereabouts of his long-lost brother. I will personally see that any further celebration is kept within bounds.' Noah paused to let that sink in. 'Do you have a room?'

The manager nodded and signalled to the desk clerk before going back into his office.

Noah took the precaution of returning to the shipyard. He had serious doubts that Bill and Fred together, but unsponsored, would be allowed into the hotel. He was just in time to intercept them. Bill was carrying a wooden trunk on his shoulder and talking non-stop. Even at a distance, Noah could see differences between them. Fred was just as tall but more finely drawn than his brother. The way he moved was less lumbering, and Noah had already heard the difference in their voices. Added to that, Fred was smartly dressed while Bill was wearing his slept-in suit.

Noah told them he had booked another room, but Fred had an urgent errand to carry out first. As they changed direction, Fred explained that he had a long-standing relationship with a young lady. 'Now I have found Bill, I can ask her to marry me.'

The house Fred led them to was in a better part of the town and as they walked, Fred filled in some details. 'Ruby is the daughter of Mr Drayton, who owns the *Heron*. I jumped at the chance of transferring when I found out it was in Jamaica.'

The Draytons' house stood in its own small plot of land, neatly fenced and surrounded by a well-kept garden. 'Please wait here,' Fred said when they reached the gate. He walked up the path, knocked at the door and was admitted.

'Why couldn't we go in with him?' Bill asked.

'I can think of two reasons,' Noah replied. 'Firstly, three or more at a proposal of marriage is too many. And you look like a tramp.' Noah shook his head. 'Didn't you undress at all last night?'

Fred was gone for nearly half an hour. When he emerged, he was waved on his way by a pleasant-looking young woman with a stern-looking man at her shoulder.

Fred was beaming. 'She said yes and you are invited to dinner.' He looked at his brother dubiously. 'Don't worry,' Noah reassured him. 'We can get him tidied up.'

The operation took a team effort. Noah arranged for their suits to be sponged and pressed. Although he had not slept in his, Noah had been wearing the suit for a week. He also found Bill a clean neckcloth.

'I can't go,' Bill groaned when he heard Mr Drayton was also a magistrate. 'He'll never let Fred marry his daughter if he finds out about me.'

'Stop worrying. He knows all about you.' To Noah, Fred confided, 'Bill always was a worrier. Mum had to keep telling him he was doing his best, working all hours to keep a roof over our heads.'

'Weren't much of a roof. And I lost you that.'

Noah insisted on taking a cab back to the Draytons' home. He was not sure Bill would not bolt if given the chance.

Bill's nervousness actually worked to their advantage. In any tricky situation, Bill retired into his shell, hardly speaking and watching Noah for clues on how to act. Mrs Drayton was a kind, motherly little lady and soon summed up the situation. She drew Bill aside while Noah spoke to her husband.

Mrs Drayton was glad to avoid conversing with Noah. The Draytons had not always been rich. They came from a working-class background. As her husband prospered, Mrs Drayton had found it hard to learn gentry manners. The thought of entertaining a baron had thrown her into a panic. As a result, she had overdone the dinner arrangements.

As the most elevated gentleman present, Noah had the honour of escorting his hostess into dinner. His heart quailed at the sight of the table. It was laid as if for a banquet with silverware, flowers and a row of glasses before each plate. Noah bent to whisper in Mrs Drayton's ear. 'Dear lady, Bill is allergic to alcohol. He will drink it to be polite but it makes him ill.'

'I do not much like wine myself. I will order an alternative.' She hurried away and soon returned carrying a jug of lemonade. Noah wondered why she did not just tell a servant.

Despite the elaborate table, the meal was served by a single maid, with Mrs Drayton and Ruby leaving the table at the end of each course. Mr Drayton shook his head. 'I am going to have to insist on extra staff.'

Noah had a chance to speak to Ruby later when Fred and her father went to discuss formalities. 'You must think us very odd,' she said. 'Mum does most of the cooking and I help if we have guests. She went overboard with the menu tonight.' She laughed ruefully. 'We will have to engage caterers for the wedding my dad wants. He insists on banns and all the trimmings. I think it is a lot of fuss. It is our wedding and ought to be what we want.'

All the trimmings were going to take a month at least. Noah was not willing to wait around that long. As a concession, he agreed to stay a few more days to hear the first banns read, then he, Fred and Bill would return to Laington.

Chapter 12

Lois was genuinely pleased that Bill was to be reunited with his brother at last. As she saw the men on their way to Plymouth, she also felt a slight feeling of relief. She had been dreading the questions she knew Noah would ask when they were alone. Perhaps, by the time they returned, Noah would be too busy preparing to leave to worry about her.

Lois's relief evaporated at the thought. What would she do? What would he decide to do about Laington? She squared her shoulders and tackled one problem at a time.

There were appointments to cancel without any idea if they would be renewed. A room had to be prepared for Bill's brother, who would presumably return with them. And today she had a meeting with the Ladies Charitable Committee. She dealt with the letters first.

It was a depressing chore. Every cancellation underlined the thought of Noah leaving. She was often exasperated with his timekeeping, constantly worried about his decision to leave and curious as to the reason for his departure.

The last she could partially understand. How would she feel about leaving Laington?

Devastated. Home was where the heart was.

But she would miss him. Was missing him already. When had his presence become so important that she looked forward to seeing him in the role of Baron? Noah played his part so well no one would guess it was just an act. At times she even thought he was coming around to the idea of staying.

And she liked him. She liked him very much. Too much for her peace of mind.

Lois shook off her gloomy thoughts and set about her other tasks.

The Ladies' committee meeting did little to raise her spirits. As soon as she arrived at the church hall, Mrs Grainger drew her to one side.

'Lois, I must tell you that Clive is most unhappy about you sharing a home with a single man. He thinks you should have a chaperone to protect your reputation.'

Lois swallowed her annoyance. 'I believe my reputation is well established,' she said firmly and walked away. What she really wanted to say was that it was no business of Clive's or anyone else's. In a house the size of Laington and surrounded by staff, they were hardly living in close proximity. Noah has never made any attempt to engage in a close relationship. Quite the opposite. He guarded his privacy every bit as carefully as she guarded hers.

It was not a comfortable meeting. Mrs Grainger, as usual, challenged every suggestion from the other members. She would argue the pros and cons and, if the suggestion was finally accepted, managed to make it seem that it was her idea. Today's topic was the distribution of Easter baskets to poor families. It was a long-established tradition that really did not need much discussion at all. All the members contributed or collected items for the baskets and Lois delivered them. 'I will do it for you this year, Lois,' Mrs Grainger declared. 'You have guests.'

'Thank you for the offer,' Lois replied politely. 'I am never too busy to carry on the tradition started by Lady Laing so many years ago. And may I remind you, Lord Laing is not a guest.' Before Mrs Grainger could respond, Lois closed the meeting.

'What a cheek,' Hattie huffed on the way home. 'She would take over the chair if we did not all vote for you to continue,' she said crossly.

Hattie was an active member of the charity, along with others from a cross-section of the community. Mrs Grainger had tried to oppose Hattie's election onto the committee and resented her presence, although she was never actually rude.

Lois started to laugh. 'How would you like to become my chaperone?' Hattie joined in the amusement when Lois finished the story. 'That would worry them even more!'

It was not really funny. In fact, it was a depressing reminder that she would have no need of a chaperone when Noah left.

As the days passed, Lois found it hard to maintain her usual calm demeaner. The daily routine seemed to throw up more and more questions. She had grown used to consulting Noah and frequently accepted his suggestions. He was more than capable of taking over completely if he wished.

That was the problem. Noah did not want Laington. It was the only reason Lois had not suggested giving up her trusteeship.

The evenings were worse. A solitary dinner and an hour or so to fill before bedtime only underlined the men's absence.

Even the Easter celebrations could not raise Lois's spirits. The vicar's sermon focused on hope, rebirth and new beginnings. None of which seemed to be on Lois's horizon in a positive way. Either she would carry on as usual or, if Noah decided to sell the estate, she'd need to build a new life alone.

Hattie's forecast for the future did not help. She had been spending a lot of time with Bill and had hopes of a proposal. 'When the silly chump stops thinking he is not good enough for me.' She even suggested that Lois might marry Noah and come to Australia with them.

There was no hope of a proposal for Lois. Noah had commitments on the other side of the world. What they were had not been mentioned but he deemed them more important than the future of Laington.

Laington's future had been the core of George's existence. He had never thought of the estate as his, saying many times that he had no right to it. It had to be kept in the best condition for Ernest or his descendants. He had passed that duty on to Lois.

She had taken it on willingly, as a temporary measure, and rather enjoyed it. Now it seemed a burden she could not shed.

If only Noah had come into his inheritance eagerly. He was more than capable of assuming control, had he wished. Lois enjoyed seeing him in the role of Baron. People accepted and liked him. She liked him.

Lois was alarmed to think her liking for Noah might be something much more. She had to remind herself again and again that she did not want to remarry. But if Noah proposed...?

Lois tried to block the idea from her mind. By the end of the week, another thought was taking root.

How long did it take to meet Fred Norton? Noah had not expected to be away for more than a day or two. He had not written to tell her why they were delayed. Not that he was obliged to, of course, Lois reminded herself. He was free to come and go as he pleased.

Go. That was the crux of the matter. Had he decided to leave for Australia immediately?

Lois could not believe he would act that way. Chiding herself for being silly, she went to check their rooms. A few clothes remained and one rather battered valise. Things that Noah could well afford to replace. The master suite had not felt so empty since George's death.

When ten days had passed, Lois accepted that Noah was not coming back. She went up to his bedroom and touched the pillow like a love-sick maiden. Had she expected to feel a sense of his head having lain there? Common sense ought to have reminded her that the linen had been changed. She went to stand at the window, staring at the empty drive until a tear trickled down her cheek and jerked her out of her trance. With a heavy heart she turned away. Had she been unscrupulous enough to search, Lois might have found something to put her mind at ease.

True to form, Noah's return took Lois by surprise. She was in her office, going through one of the household accounts, when she heard voices in the hall. One familiar voice propelled out of her chair and into the hall. She stared at Noah for an instant and when he opened his arms, she flew into them without hesitation. He held her close and kissed her until they were both dizzy.

Cheering brought Lois back to her senses. Bill and his alter ego were grinning and clapping their hands. Pound stood to one side with a benign smile. She took a quick step back. Whatever had come over her? 'Welcome home, my lord,' was the best she could manage.

'Hope I get a welcome like that,' Bill chuckled.

Noah rescued Lois by introducing Fred.

Had she not been expecting him, Lois might have thought she was seeing double. The introduction allowed her time to gather her scattered wits. Slipping into her role of hostess, she welcomed Fred, asked after their journey, said how pleased the brothers must be and a string of other inanities. Through it all she avoided looking at Noah.

Proud coughed. 'Shall I show Mr Norton to his room?'

'Nah,' Bill cut in. 'I'll take him up. We'll leave these two to finish their welcome.' He took Fred by the arm and headed for the stairs. With one foot on the first step, he turned back to ask Lois. 'Where have you put him?'

'The next room to yours.'

Lois would have followed them but Noah caught her hand and almost dragged her into the drawing room. With the door safely closed, he pulled her back into his arms. 'Shall we?' he murmured as he bent his head.

Lois wriggled free, blushing. 'I'm sorry,' she muttered. 'I don't know what came over me.'

'I thought you were glad to see me.'

'I am. I thought you had gone back to Australia.' That revealed too much. To cover her confusion, she went on the attack. 'You always take me by surprise. You did not write to say when to expect you.'

She looked adorable and Noah, with laughing eyes, reached out.

Lois scooted away, behind a sofa. Noah made to move around it and Lois pulled a chair into his path. Side to side they tried to catch or avoid and did not hear Pound enter the room. He gave his attention-seeking cough and they turned like naughty children. Lois took advantage of Noah's temporary distraction to scoot behind him and out of the door.

Noah smiled at the butler and followed her more slowly.

Lois did not stop running until she was safely in her parlour. She leant back against the door, reliving the last few minutes. 'Dear Heaven,' she whispered. 'What have I done?' The answer did not need words. She had fallen in love. When or how it had happened she did not know. She had not known what falling in love felt like.

Lois went through to her bedroom. This was one situation she could not talk over with George's picture. It was a situation she was going to have to discuss with Noah. Just not yet.

Chapter 13

Lois stayed in her room until the dinner gong sounded. She opened her door a crack and listened for the sound of Bill and Fred leaving their rooms before she stepped out into the passage.

'I hope you found your room comfortable, Mr Norton,' she said as they met at the head of the stairs.

'Yes, thank you, Mrs Laing. It is sheer luxury after a ship's cabin.'

'Aw, come on!' Bill laughed. 'We don't do that Mr and Mrs stuff.'

'There is no need for formality,' Lois told Fred. 'I feel as though I know you already. Please call me Lois.'

As they reached the hall, Noah emerged from the drawing room. He had come down early in the hope of catching Lois alone. She was listening to Bill and studiously avoiding Noah's eyes. Noah sighed. He would have to wait until after dinner.

Bill had picked up on the strained atmosphere and put it down to shyness. That kiss had been very public, not at all the way Lois usually behaved. He would help her out.

'Do we go straight in to dinner?' he asked before turning to Fred. 'We use the small dining room now.' Without permission, he led the way.

Lois had no choice but to fall in behind, with Noah close to her side. His hand seemed to burn through her clothes as he held her chair while she sat.

There was no lack of conversation over the meal. Fred, encouraged by Bill and Noah, was happy to tell her how he had spent the years of separation. Noah had heard most of it on the journey from Bristol and was happy to watch Lois interact with the brothers.

Lois was happy to let Fred talk. He was very like Bill physically, but their different experiences had given Fred a degree of polish.

'After Mum and Lucy died, I ran away,' Fred began. He had been taken in by a gentleman who had a place for homeless boys.

They were housed, fed and educated. 'When I was fourteen, I was apprenticed into the navy.'

'That would not have suited Noah,' Bill said, chuckling, and the talk switched to Bill and Noah's journey. From then until the end of the meal, the conversation was mostly about the three men's various travels.

'That was how I met Ruby,' Fred told them. It was the first Lois had heard about the recent visit to Bristol. As the story unfolded, Lois found that the men would not be leaving Laington for some time.

Fred continued. 'Ruby is the daughter of Mr Drayton, who owns the Heron. We met years ago at a civic reception. I was there as an usher and general dogsbody. Ruby had accompanied her father. She does not like parties very much and we found a quiet corner and got talking.' He beamed at Lois. 'We are going to get married and go to Australia with Noah and Bill.'

Lois said congratulations. 'You are invited to the wedding,' Fred added.

Lois tried to protest. 'That is unnecessary. I do not know the Draytons.' She was overruled. 'You are like part of the family,' Bill insisted. 'Tell her she has to come, Noah.'

Noah was not sure his wishes held much sway with Lois, but the brothers were so adamant on her attending the wedding, he was spared the effort.

As soon as the meal was over, Bill said he was taking Fred to meet Hattie.

'There might be another wedding in the offing,' Noah said after the men left. He moved to help Lois rise from her chair and felt her quiver when his hand touched her arm. 'We need to talk, Lois,' he said quietly. 'It is unfortunate I had to leave before we resolved the matter of those letters.'

Lois accompanied him into the drawing room. The letters were a touchy subject but less unwelcome than discussing her behaviour on his arrival.

Lois did not sit down and kept a distance between them. Noah took a paper from his pocket and handed it to her.

Lois moved closer to a lamp to read. The sight of George's spidery writing brought a lump to her throat. His hands had become very unsteady towards the end. She glanced at the bottom of the page. George had had a quirky habit of dating his letters after his signature. It was, as Noah had insisted, just over two years ago.

Lois read the letter through. It was a poignant appeal from a sick man at the end of his tether. I have lost my wife and my children. I rely on Lois, my daughter-in-law, but we need you now while I have the strength to teach you how to be a gentleman. If you receive this, please come. You are the next baron and Laington needs you.

Lois could not contain her tears. George had been a proud man. Being forced to beg showed how desperate he had become.

Noah could not see her face, but her heaving shoulders told him she was crying. Hesitantly, he guided her onto a nearby sofa and sat beside her. He would have liked to take her into his arms but contented himself with offering his clean handkerchief.

Lois mopped her face and looked at him. 'I did not know about this.' She lifted the letter. 'I helped with George's correspondence but I did not know he had written this. I owe you an apology.'

'That does not matter now. I am sorry you were left to carry on alone.'

Lois looked back at the letter. There were instructions on how to proceed and the name of a Sydney solicitor. She shook her head sadly. 'It would have relieved George's mind to know that you did not need to be taught your manners.'

Noah gave a small laugh. 'I have to admit that bit rankled.' They were talking at last and Noah decided now was the time to explain his late arrival.

'Lois, I could not come immediately. Gramp had suffered a heart attack. My wife was expecting a child. It was unthinkable to subject her to a long voyage. I could not leave my mother wither the double responsibility.'

Lois startled. 'You are married?'

'No.' Noah shook his head and sighed. 'Clara was having a hard time. She hated living on a remote station and cried all the time. By the time the child was born, she had lost the will to live.'

Lois could understand his dilemma. 'She died.' It was not really a question.

Noah nodded and took a deep breath. 'The child survived. I have a daughter. It was a living nightmare.' Noah bent forward over the hands he had clasped between his knees. His voice was low. 'I had to take her to her maternal aunt in Adelaide. I only had the help of an aboriginal woman. My mother could not feed her and had her hands full looking after Gramp.'

Lois did not know what to say. Sorry was inadequate and further questions would be intrusive. She said sorry anyway.

'So, there you have it. Gramp died just before Christmas.'

Lois repeated her apology. 'You were very fond of your grandfather.' She did not dare to ask how fond he had been of his wife.

Noah smiled sadly. 'He was more of a father than my own had ever been.' He glanced at Lois. 'Much the same as you were fond of George. I am sorry I never got to meet him.'

Lois nodded. 'He would have liked you. He often spoke of Ernest but worried that you would follow in his, well, somewhat erratic footsteps.'

'He never changed.' Noah's mind drifted off. Lois sat quietly, watching the changing expressions on his face. As though talking to himself, Noah relived his memories. 'Right to the end Gramp would not give up his tobacco and whiskey. Minutes before he died, he said he was dying of a tot! It was the last thing that touched his lips apart from a whispered "Jenna is waiting."'

The name rang a bell. 'Jenna was your grandmother.'

'Yes. I don't recall ever meeting her but she was the love of Gramp's life.' Noah twisted the gold ring on his right hand. 'She had this made from the only gold nugget Gramp ever found. My mother knew her and said she was as adventurous as Gramp. My father called them irresponsible gypsies.'

'Do you know why your grandfather left England?'

'No, he just said he was deported and laughed. He was always laughing.'

'Ernest eloped with a married woman, Jenna Matthews.'

Noah gave a roar of laughter. 'The old rogue. He didn't tell me that bit.' Still smiling, Noah continued. 'He only spoke of

Laington after I received George's letter. Just before he died his mind was wandering, mixing up the past and present. We were talking about my father, a very rare occurrence. Apparently, my father had called him a selfish bastard. I can hear Gramp chuckling as he said he was not the only one as he had never gotten around to marrying Jenna!'

'I think I would have liked Ernest. George did and tried for years to find him. Even before it became urgent.'

They shared memories of the two beloved old men, more in harmony than at any time in their acquaintance.

The mood was broken when Bill rushed into the room. 'I'm going to marry Hattie!'

Fred entered more slowly. 'Would you believe he' – he pointed a thumb at his brother – 'proposed while I was sitting there!'

'What did Hattie say – beyond yes?'

Fred shook his head. 'She told him he had taken his time about it!'

Lois rang for the evening refreshment and they toasted the two couples with cups of tea.

When Lois decided to retire, Noah walked with her to the door. At the foot of the stairs, she turned back. 'Would you like to see the other letters? I removed them from the study when I cleared George's things.' At Noah's nod, she went to fetch them.

Noah waited in the hall until Lois returned. She carried a leather case, which she held out to him. 'Read them at your leisure, but I would like them back.'

Noah reached out with both hands. One took hold of the case and the other her wrist. 'Do I get a goodnight kiss?'

Lois reared back, tugging to free her wrist. 'No, no,' she stammered. 'That was a mistake. It must not happen again.' With a mighty effort, she pulled free and ran up the stairs.

Noah sighed. Perhaps she was right. There was no point in starting a relationship that had no future.

Chapter 14

Noah took the case up to the study. It was quite heavy and he might need to use the desk. He brought a lamp through from the bedroom and sat down to read.

The case contained a number of labelled folders. Noah withdrew the one marked 'Ernest' and set the case aside. A quick glance showed that the letters were filed in chronological order with the most recent on top. The first letter was from Richard Harris, writing to inform Lois that the new baron had arrived and was not happy about the trustee situation. Noah had to smile at the guarded comment. Had Lois been expecting an angry as well as an uncouth man? It would explain her initial wariness.

Noah flicked past a number of official-looking documents until he found the letter he was seeking. As Lois had said, it was dated just over five years ago. It was unlike his letter, clearly written and much more impersonal. Noah glossed over the first section, which mentioned previous letters, and his eyes fastened on the words 'You are heir to the barony.' Noah frowned. That implied Simon Laing had already died. From the tone of his own letter, Noah had assumed it was written in the throes of recent loss. The writing was different too. Not just in its neatness but in completely different hand.

Noah laid it aside. The next letter was from a solicitor in Sydney and gave details of Ernest and Noah Laing's last known address. *Working on a sheep farm.* That did not tell the whole story. They had been owners for at least two years before that. It gave the impression that they had been reduced to the rank of labourers.

Attached to the letter was a lengthy report of the alleged search. Apart from a newspaper cutting of his father's death in a pub brawl and the date of Grandma Jenna's death, the rest was pure fiction. Yes, they had visited some of the places mentioned, but the dates did not match. It was as though the investigator had laid out a map and picked names at random. The size of the fee he had claimed was far more than he deserved.

The investigator had drawn his inspiration from the next letter in the pile. This was a commission to search for the whereabouts of Earnest Joseph Laing or any relatives. It mentioned that Ernest had arrived in Australia around 1797/98 and was known to have moved about.

Further back in the folder were similar letters to solicitors and investigators in various parts of Australia. They only said the matter concerned an inheritance. Very few of these had received any response.

At the very back of the folder were school reports and award certificates in Ernest's name. Noah smiled. Even as a boy, Gramp had been a handful! He'd excelled at maths but had not applied himself to subjects that had not interested him. His awards were all for sporting events.

Noah started to tidy the papers away when another letter slipped out. It was from a Colonel James and was dated more than forty years ago. Noah only bothered to look closer when his eye caught Ernest's name. He read it through several times and finally sat back with a sigh.

George had tried to find Ernest through the agency of a mutual acquaintance who was going to Australia. The colonel said he had been unable to locate Ernest or deliver the letter. He promised to continue the search as and when he could, keeping the letter safe in the hope of delivering it at a later date.

Reading the letters had answered some of Noah's questions and raised even more. Foremost in his mind was one of Gramp's rambling comments. *Tell George I am sorry I did not write.* Did that mean he had received a letter and not replied? He would never know.

Noah put the folder back into the case and went to bed.

His last waking thought was of kissing Lois. With hindsight it had been a mistake. He had resolved not to get involved but her greeting has been spontaneous. And she had seemed to enjoy the kiss as much as he had. Then, when they'd said goodnight, she had shied away. Pity.

The kiss was also on Lois's mind. She had never experienced anything like it. For as long as it had lasted, she had only been aware of Noah and the sensation of floating in a cloud of happiness. She ought to wish it had never happened, but she would treasure the moment. Though it must not happen again. She loved Noah and could hardly contemplate his leaving. One experience she could remember and treasure. Building on it would be a disaster.

Chapter 15

Next morning, Noah came down later than usual for breakfast. With any luck Bill and Fred would have finished and gone about their own business. Luck was not with him as Fred was not such an early riser as his brother, and they met Noah at the top of the stairs. Bill led the way to the small dining room and made straight for the buffet.

'You can't start without Lois,' Fred said sharply.

'You may eat when you please,' Noah told him. 'Breakfast is always informal.' Noah went back into the hall, ignoring Bill's puzzled call, 'Aren't you eating?'

Lois was just descending the stairs and stopped at the sight of him.

She had lain awake for a long time last night, mulling over how she should treat Noah. There was no denying she had enjoyed their kiss and then rebuffed him as they said goodnight. She could not tell him how tempting it had been to accept. The temptation had still been there when she awoke. How was she to spend time with him without giving in?

She had delayed coming down in the hope that she could speak to him alone. Bill could be relied upon to appear for breakfast at the earliest possible moment, presumably bringing Fred with him.

Noah was standing in the hall, and she stilled. Oh, what a pleasure it would be to fly down into his arms. *Stop that*, she told herself sharply and put on a bright smile. 'Have you finished breakfast?' she asked, coming to join him.

'No, the others are in there.' He nodded to the dining room. 'But we need to talk.'

Lois led the way to her office and they stood facing each other, neither knowing how to start. Noah took a deep breath. 'About that kiss. It cannot be forgotten but I assure you it will not happen again.' It ought to have been reassuring, but Lois felt a deep disappointment. Perhaps it had not been so wonderful for him.

'I agree,' Lois said. 'I don't know what came over me.' She went towards the door and said briskly, 'Now, with that out of the way, shall we join the brothers?'

Noah followed more slowly. Lois was so matter of fact. Perhaps her welcome had just been a mixture of surprise and relief. She had admitted wondering if he was going to return. Her later refusal to repeat the kiss seemed to imply that she had not enjoyed the kiss as much as he had. It was a lowering thought. He was out of practice, but she had felt so right in his arms.

Lois and Noah managed to get through the day's routine in apparent harmony. The managers' meeting was long and they had to focus on the reports. The quarry manager asked Noah to come and inspect progress on the new rail link, and the buildings manager asked Noah to study the estimates for repairs to the mill.

Lois urged Noah to go to the quarry, saying, 'You know more about railways than I do.' She was relieved when he agreed. It got him out of the house and they did not meet again until dinner time.

The presence of Bill and Fred eased the atmosphere over dinner, but they did not come to the drawing room. Noah had remembered his duties as a host and took the brothers off to the games room to play billiards. Lois ought to have been relieved but, quite unfairly, felt peeved that he was avoiding her. After an hour of making a mess of her embroidery, she went up to her room.

Over the next few days, Lois found plenty of opportunities to avoid Noah. She spent time with Hattie, checked all the household linens with Mrs Collins and the store cupboards with Pound and the cook. In desperation she decided to wash the precious china ornaments collected by George's first wife. Her excuse was that she did not like to place the responsibility for any breakages on the maids and she enjoyed handling the delicate pieces. It also kept her mind from wondering what Noah was doing.

Noah understood Lois's tactics. The presence of Fred Norton gave him the opportunity to do the same. Now he was assured of his brother's safety, Bill had more or less abandoned him and went back to working around the estate. Their different experiences meant they had little in common. Fred had no interest in animals and did not ride, so it was left to Noah to find ways of filling the man's time. Fortunately, they shared an interest in art. Drawing was one of the things Fred had been able to do on his long voyages, and he offered to show Noah his sketch books. That led to tours of the house, studying the various pictures. As a consequence, Noah came to know more about the house and contents than he had ever intended.

Gramp had warned him not to be seduced by Laington. He had called it a prison disguised as a palace. It lured you in and made you a prisoner. Noah had no fear of that. He could admire the various artifacts, but they held no meaning for him. Ironically, he had been seduced by Lois, who wanted nothing to do with him.

One day Lois was pretending to be busy writing letters when there was a bustle of activity in the hall. Lois went to investigate and saw her dear friend, Mary Latimer, removing her cloak and gloves.

'Mary!' Lois cried, rushing forward. 'I did not know you were visiting.'

'More than that, I hope,' Mary said, giving Lois a hug. 'I have come seeking sanctuary. I knew you would not mind us descending upon you.' Mary gave Lois another hug and a rueful smile. 'Mama keeps interfering in the nursery regime and upsetting Nanny. Clive has a face as long as a wet weekend and Irene keeps on about the baron. Where is he?'

Lois could not reply immediately as Nanny, carrying a crying baby, and Mary's maid were being escorted through the door by the Grainger's coachman.

'Of course you may stay,' Lois said, beckoning Pound. 'Have the nursery prepared as soon as possible. Mrs Latimer will have the room next to mine.'

News of the arrivals had spread through the house and Mrs Collins hurried forward. 'Perhaps Nanny might like to come to my parlour while the nursery is prepared. Poor baby sounds quite distressed.' Mary nodded and Nanny went with the housekeeper.

Mary linked her arm through Lois's. 'Quiet at last!' With the familiarity of long friendship, Mary more or less dragged Lois into the drawing room. Once the door was shut, she demanded, 'Now, tell me all about the mystery man. Your letters hinted at some problem.'

Lois sat beside her friend. 'He does not intend to stay.'

'What! Is he another one who wants to spend all his time in London, leaving you to do all the work?'

'No, he has commitments in Australia. He owns a huge sheep station.' Lois could not bring herself to mention his daughter. She could not discuss his private life even with Mary.

'What is he going to do about Laington?'

'I don't know.'

Mary had inherited her mother's forceful nature, although she tempered it with tact. She had spent her girlhood smoothing the feathers her mother had ruffled and found an appealing smile got things done much more efficiently. This was a situation that needed sorting. 'It seems I have come just in time.'

Lois laughed. Mary would not be put off with evasions. It was cowardly but Lois was quite prepared to let her friend probe where she did not dare.

The subject of their conversation ended the meeting by coming into the drawing room to be introduced. As far as anyone knew, he was the baron and would expect to meet any visitors. One look at the visitor and his spirits sank. She was an older version of Irene Grainger and was looking back at him with an expectant smile.

'Mary, may I introduce Lord Noah Laing,' Lois said brightly. 'Noah, this is my friend, Mrs Mary Latimer. She has come to stay for a while.'

Noah stifled a groan and came forward to shake her hand. 'Welcome to Laington, Mrs Latimer. I am pleased to meet any friend of Lois's.'

Mary laughed softly. 'You may change your mind when I monopolise her company. We have not seen each other for many months and have a lot to catch up on. But I am pleased to meet you, too. How are you enjoying being a baron?'

'It feels strange,' Noah admitted.

Mary nodded. 'Lois wrote to say you had arrived but knew very little about your life in Australia. Won't you sit down and tell me about it?'

With subtle questions, Mary manoeuvred Noah into a description of his sheep station.

'Who is looking after it now?' Mary asked. She smiled impishly. 'Have you left someone as capable as Lois in charge?'

'I doubt anyone is as capable as Lois,' Noah replied gallantly. Then he went on to tell them about David Owen, his manager, who was also his stepfather. This was news to Lois. She had deliberately not asked such questions in case it heightened Noah's urge to return promptly.

'Well, that must be a relief to you.' Mary sat back as though well satisfied. 'Now you can take the responsibility for Laington from Lois's shoulders.' Before he could make any reply, Mary continued. 'She will never complain. For as long as I have known her, Lois has been put upon.'

'Mary,' Lois protested. 'That was never the case!'

Mary snorted. 'I don't know how you can say that. Lady Charlotte loaded you with all the things she could not be bothered with and took all the credit. And Simon, well, the less said the better!'

Noah had an uneasy feeling. He could not put his finger on it but he was sure he was being given a subtle hint.

The conversation was brought to a close by a maid coming with a message from Nanny. 'Please will Mrs Latimer come now. Master Alex needs his mama.'

Mary groaned. 'Oh, Lord, it is that time again.' She stood up to follow the maid. 'Please excuse me. The joys of motherhood are vastly overrated.'

'Alex is Mary's baby son. I have not met him yet.' Lois smiled. 'It will be strange to have a baby in the nursery.' Lois watched Noah's face for any sign that he was missing his own daughter.

Noah walked about the room trying to think of a suitable comment. As he passed the window, he spotted two horses coming up the drive. The vicar was in the lead, with Clive Grainger in close pursuit.

'You have more visitors. Mr Grainger and the vicar,' Noah said wearily.

Lois wrinkled her nose. 'Mary came to me to escape her family. I am surprised Mrs Grainger has not come too.'

Pound announced the callers and was almost jostled out of the way by Clive. He gave Noah a frosty stare. 'I would like to speak to Lois alone, my lord.'

'By all means.' Noah was glad to turn to the vicar. 'If you do not have urgent business with Mrs Laing, perhaps you would like to join me elsewhere?'

'It is you I have come to see, Lord Laing.' The vicar looked uneasy and after a sorrowful nod to Lois, followed Noah from the room.

As soon as the door was closed, Clive rushed forward and took Lois's hands.

'My dear Lois. I hardly know how to tell you.'

Lois tugged her hands free and moved away. It was unusual for Clive to show such hesitation. 'Whatever is the matter?'

'I am not one to gossip but I have heard the most disturbing rumour. It is all over town that the baron intends to return to Australia.'

Oh, Lord, Lois thought. How had that got out? Trying to look surprised, Lois replied, 'Where did you hear that?'

Clive avoided her eyes. 'One just hears things. People talk and one cannot help overhearing. What will you do?'

'Nothing,' Lois said sharply. 'I am surprised you would repeat it.'

It was not the reaction Clive had hoped for. He launched into his prepared speech of support and a renewal of his proposals. His mother had been certain that Lois would be distraught and turn to a loyal friend. He did not like to contemplate telling her she was wrong.

Lois wanted Clive gone. 'If that is all, I will not detain you any longer. I am sure you can find your own way out.' Lois turned her back on him. She ignored his mumbled protests and moved to look out of the window, willing him to leave. He was taking a long time about it, but Lois refused to turn around. She was angry. How dare he interfere? She could hear Clive shuffling his feet and wondered how long it would take him to go. She heard the door open and Pound's polite cough.

'Mrs Laing, the baron has asked for you to join him and the vicar in your office.'

Lois sailed past Clive without a glance and hurried across the hall. Noah met her at the door and ushered her inside. The vicar was standing by the desk, twisting his hat between his hands.

'The vicar has come to inform me that a rumour is abroad about my intention to leave.'

Lois sank into her chair behind the desk. 'Mr Grainger came on the same errand.'

Noah invited the vicar to take a seat. 'There is truth in the rumour. I have commitments in Australia. Mrs Laing is aware of this. How and when I leave is my business.'

The young vicar shook his head. 'I am sorry to hear that. I do not usually give credence to gossip but several people have come to me with their concerns.'

'It is a pity they have nothing else to talk about,' Noah said testily. 'Mrs Laing foresaw this situation and we have tried to avoid any agitation. When I leave, they will soon settle down.'

The vicar stood up. 'Thank you for being open with me, my lord. I shall try to quell any comments I hear.' He bowed to Lois and Noah opened the door for him to leave.

'I wonder how the news got out,' Lois wondered aloud. She shrugged. 'I suppose it was inevitable. I think you said you had warned Bill not to say anything but with his and Hattie's wedding coming up and their move to Australia, I suppose people just put two and two together.'

Noah frowned. 'Did you say Mr Grainger came on the same errand?'

'Yes,' Lois said and tightened her lips in annoyance. 'I sent him away quite sharply. How dare he!'

Noah had to smile. Lois seldom showed her feelings and was now almost twitching with anger. He would have liked to change the subject but there was still the matter of how to deal with the gossip.

'Other people are talking too,' he reminded her.

Lois shrugged. 'If they dare to ask me, I shall refer them to you.' She tilted her head and waited for his reply.

Noah mimicked her shrug. 'If they dare to ask me, I shall stare back until they back off. I have found silence is more dismissing than words.'

Lois started to laugh. 'That is exactly what I did to Clive. I turned my back waiting for him to take the hint.' She looked at Noah. 'I hope he did leave and is not still lingering in the drawing room.'

'Pound will have seen him off the premises,' Noah reassured her. 'On a brighter subject, Mrs Latimer did not seem overly keen to see her child.'

'I am sure Mary loves him but she did not have a very good example in her mother. Children were necessary but they are generally left in the care of a nanny until they are old enough to be interesting. My memories of my own mother are vague. I know she was pretty but I don't think she spent very much time with me. After my father died, Mama went into a decline.' Lois smiled sadly. 'At least I had George and Sarah.'

'If Mrs Grainger had been my mother, I would not have wanted to spend much time with her,' Noah said laughingly.

'What about your mother?' It was the most personal question Lois had ever asked, and Noah was happy to reply.

'My mother endured years of trailing around the country to be with me. I only found out it had been a trial when we settled at the farm. Ma has a talent for making a home wherever we happened to be.' He chuckled. 'It might be for only a few days, possibly in a tent, or for several months in an hotel. Then we packed up again and were on the move.'

'I have never been anywhere for more than a week or so.' Lois looked up and wished she had not. Noah's face wore an odd expression of… Lois could not quite put a name to it – surprise, consideration and a softening of his lips that could have been pity.

'Not that I minded,' Lois hurried to reassure him. 'Everything I loved was here.'

It was on the tip of Noah's tongue to ask if that included her husband. Mrs Latimer had mentioned him with distain. Come to think of it, Simon Laing was seldom mentioned by anyone. The only time Noah had asked about him, Lois had retreated into her shell. It was none of his business but it was becoming important. A fact that irked him.

They had fallen silent, each with their own thoughts. Lois wondered if Noah was thinking of his home, his mother and his daughter. Had it been a wrench to leave them? He had been surprised at Mary's lack of maternal interest. It made his wish to return home understandable. Home was where you loved and were loved.

And you love Noah, said the voice in her heart. Lois pushed the thought aside and stood up. 'I must go to check on the nursery.' She hurried from the room, trying to outrun the thought that she was going to be very lonely when he left.

Chapter 16

Lois did not need to check the nursery. Mrs Collins could be relied upon to see that even the seldom used rooms were cleaned and aired on a regular basis. Lois just wanted to see the baby.

Lois entered the nursery quietly. Nanny was tidying away a bowl and the other paraphernalia of an infant's toilet and turned with a smile. She was quite young and Mary had written that Nanny had very modern ideas, the main cause of her disagreements with Mrs Gardner.

'I have just put Master Alex down for a sleep,' she whispered. 'Fed and cleaned. He will soon get over the journey.'

'May I take a peep?' Lois asked. 'I won't disturb him.' Just

Nanny opened the door to the night nursery and stood aside for Lois to approach the crib. The child was sucking one fist, behind which Lois was sure she could see a smile. At four months old, Alex still had the bland, unformed features of the newborn. Lois had always wondered at doting parents saying the child resembled its mother, father or other relative.

Lois loved children. On her visits she usually manged to cuddle a baby or spend a few minutes with the older children. Children were so uncomplicated. They responded to any overture of friendship and it was only as they grew older that they learned the artifice of using that friendship for gain.

Lois crept away. 'Thank you. I will come back when Alex is awake. He looks very contented now.'

Nanny chuckled. 'He can be quite demanding and protests loudly if his needs are not immediately met.'

'Do you have everything you need?'

'Thank you, yes. Mrs Collins has assigned a girl to wait on us.'

With everything in order, Lois went back downstairs.

Pound met her in the hall to announce that the gentlemen had all gone out. 'Lord Laing sends his apologies.' That rather implied that Bill and Fred had not bothered with the courtesy. Pound ensured Mr Norton, and now his brother, were treated respectfully, but neither ranked very highly in Pound's esteem. 'Lady Latimer is in the drawing room.'

Lois joined her friend and they went through to lunch. 'This is just like old times,' Mary said as she helped herself from the buffet. 'Although I liked it when we were young and ate in the nursery.' Mary shuddered. 'Now the nursery is where Alex eats me.'

'You are still feeding him yourself?' It was not really a question. Mary had written that she did not enjoy nursing but Nanny had insisted. Nanny – Lois had never heard her referred to by name – had come highly recommended and Mary did not want to lose her.

'Not for much longer,' Mary said. 'Nanny is starting to wean him onto a bottle. It cannot be soon enough for me. I only gave in because Nanny said it would help me to get my figure back.' Mary sat back to display her tiny waist. 'Not quite back to twenty-five inches but corsets help.'

Mary had changed from her arrival clothes into a becoming gown of figured silk. She studied Lois critically. 'You have let yourself go, Lois. I am sure you have had that dress for years.'

Lois never gave a great deal of thought to her clothes. Unless it was a special occasion, she just wore the garments Sarah laid out for her. They always suited her agenda, whether it was visiting sites around the estate or making more formal calls. Today she was wearing a plain grey gown with a white lace collar. 'I don't have many occasions to dress up for,' she said defensively. 'But I must renew my wardrobe soon.'

Lois went on to tell Mary about her invitation to Fred's wedding. That led to an account of Noah's part in helping Bill to find his brother.

Mary laughed. 'Oh, I have heard all about Mr Norton. Mama is surprised you are entertaining an ex-convict.'

'He is Noah's guest. And friend. I know it sounds odd but they have a strong bond. Bill is quite endearing in a naïve kind of way. I thought at first he was slow-witted but it is just that he has been starved of education. His brother, Fred, is much more cultured.'

Lois was happy to talk frankly with Mary. It was not gossip so much as sharing thoughts. Mary liked to keep abreast of events and any news would not be spread.

Lois had not realised how often she mentioned Noah until Mary put down her teacup and exclaimed, 'You are in love with him!'

Lois looked startled. 'With Fred Norton?'

'Silly! I mean you are in love with the reluctant baron!'

'Oh, how can you tell?'

'I have known you since we were children. You may be able to hide your feelings from other people but you don't fool me.'

'What am I going to do?' Lois sighed. 'I missed him terribly while they were searching for Fred. It will be a hundred times worse when he is gone for good.'

'You poor dear.' Mary patted Lois's hand. 'Is there no way of persuading Noah to stay? You haven't done anything, have you?'

Lois blushed and avoided Mary's shrew gaze. 'I kissed him when he came home. I don't know what came over me. I didn't stop to think. He was there and it seemed the most natural thing in the world to fly into his arms.'

Mary grinned. 'How did Noah react to that?'

'I thought he enjoyed it but he has promised it will not happen again. I know that is a wise decision but I cannot help wishing it could happen again.'

Mary tutted. 'Well, the best thing you can do is to spend as little time as possible in his company.' A reminiscence smile curved her lips. 'Temptation is hard to resist.'

Lois knew that smile. Mary wore it every time she thought of her husband. She had proudly confided that she and Lawrence had anticipated their wedding vows on several occasions. At the time, Lois had not understood why anyone would want to take on their wifely duties before they absolutely had to. Her own deflowering had been swift and painful. Simon had said it would get better, but it had not.

Lois shied away from the memory.

As a distraction, Lois picked up her cup, but they had lingered over their meal and the tea had grown cold. She pulled a face and asked if Mary wanted a fresh pot of tea.

'No, thank you. Let us go and examine your wardrobe. Getting you up to date will take some time.' Mary got to her feet. 'Come on,' she urged. 'I have never known anyone less interested in their appearance.'

Dinner that evening was a lively affair. Hattie had come to join them and Mary was fascinated by the brothers. It was not difficult to keep the conversation flowing. Mary had persuaded Lois to borrow one of her own gowns and Noah could hardly keep his eyes off her. The shimmering silk gown of green and blue echoed the colour of her eyes and the low neckline exposed more of her creamy skin. A gold locket nestled enticingly in the valley between her breasts. She was also more animated than usual, which brought a smile to her lips and a becoming glow to her cheeks.

Bill was holding the floor, enthusiastically telling Mary about the cottage and job Noah had promised him on the sheep station.

Mary switched her attention to Noah. 'What made you buy a sheep farm?'

'I did not buy it. My grandfather won it in a card game.' Mary raised her eyebrows. She had heard long ago about Ernest Laing's gambling habits. She looked quickly at Lois to see if she'd made the connection to her own father, but Lois seemed unconcerned.

'That was quite a win. Lois has told me your farm makes Laington seem like a mere puddle.'

'Mary!' Lois protested. 'I said no such thing!' Lois looked quickly at Noah. 'I just said it is much bigger than Laington.'

Noah would have changed the subject, but Mary was on the hunt for information.

'You said your stepfather is managing it while you are away. Do you have any other family?'

Lois leant forward, about to steer the conversation away. She had not told Mary about Noah's marriage or the child.

Noah was quite capable of protecting his own privacy. 'I have a mother, of course, and two stepbrothers. David Owen was already working on the sheep station when we arrived. As we were complete novices in that area, Gramp was happy to promote

David to manager. I don't think Gramp intended to stay there but his strength was failing. It did not take much persuasion to make him take life at a slower pace.'

'Did you miss the travelling?'

Noah shook his head. 'I enjoyed seeing other places but it was time to settle down.' Noah quite ruthlessly turned the tables. 'I believe you have travelled a great deal.'

'My husband was posted to Paris soon after we were married. His family have connections in the wine trade.'

'I can't drink wine,' Bill put in. 'It makes me a bit silly.'

Noah laughed aloud. 'More than a bit, my friend. Too much ale has the same effect. I thought you would get us arrested after we located Fred.' Noah went on to describe Bill's delight at finding his brother, and Mary turned her quizzing to Fred.

One topic ran into another and came to rest on the imminent weddings. 'You will need a trousseau, Hattie. I have already decided to refresh Lois's wardrobe and would be happy to advise you, too,' Mary offered.

'I don't need a trousseau,' Hattie said, laughing. 'I will have no occasion to wear fancy clothes.'

The three men groaned. 'I think it is time we left the ladies to discuss clothes,' Noah declared and looked to Lois to bring the meal to an end. Lois had been enjoying the conversations and reluctantly stood. 'Ladies, I believe the gentlemen are tired of our company.' She smiled at them all. 'I will excuse you from joining us in the drawing room.'

Noah watched her lead her friends from the room with some regret. She had not taken much part in the talk but his frequent glances had informed him that she was enjoying the company. It brought home to him that she would be very lonely when they all left. He wished she could come to Australia with them, but he had seen what happened when you uprooted a woman from her natural habitat. He had met and married Clara in Adelaide where she'd lived a very social life. She had hated the isolation of the sheep station and the absence of entertainment. Eventually it had sapped her spirit. He could not do that to Lois.

Chapter 17

In the following weeks, Noah learned the true meaning of loneliness, and it was not a lack of company. Fred had gone to spend time with his fiancée and Bill was either working or visiting Hattie. During his life, Noah had been content to spend long periods alone. Now he was surrounded by people and felt isolated.

True to her word, Mary had taken Lois in hand. When they were not visiting friends and dressmakers, the house was invaded by hordes of visitors. Noah thought that every woman of note in the community came to see Mary and baby Alex, often bringing their own children. The daily business of the estate continued as usual but there were no new invitations that included Noah.

The isolation was subtle. No one snubbed him. People spoke to him but there was a lack of interest in his opinions. The staff and tenants were polite. On his rides, people acknowledged him but never sought to engage him in conversation. Noah gradually withdrew, spending time in the study, but even there he was aware of a bustle that said others were happily going about their own business.

The only person to actively seek his company was Hattie. One day, when Noah was out riding, she hailed him from her garden and invited him into the house.

'I want to talk to you,' she said as she led him into her parlour. 'How do I go about settling Laington Grace on Lois?'

Noah was taken aback. He had been expecting a lecture. 'You have reminded me that I need to do the same with the estate. I will need to go to London to visit the solicitor.'

'Get him to come here. You may not want to be the baron but, at the moment, you are and need to act like it.' She nodded decisively. 'George always had his lawyer come to him. It is the way things are done.'

It was another area Noah had never considered. An attitude of superiority that Gramp had absorbed during his youth. Virtually homeless, he'd still had an air of command and had people responded. Not that they'd been paupers. Or idlers. They had not lived on Gramp's winnings. They worked when the opportunity offered. When they had more money in hand than needed, Gramp invested in promising schemes, more to help the tryers than in hope of reward. His Midas touch continued and he amassed a sizeable fortune. It was just possessions he despised. *Travel light*, he had always insisted. *Keep what you need and leave the rest behind.*

Hattie recalled him from his memories with a small cough. Noah apologised and returned to her original question. 'Mr Harris will be able to advise you. And there is the matter of your pension. I assume that will continue after you marry but it needs to be clarified.'

'Oh, I know what I want to do with that. I have talked it over with Bill and he wants nothing to do with it. He has his pride although he keeps it well hidden, and he said he will support me, not the other way around.'

Hattie smiled indulgently. 'I really am quite fond of him, you know. Not in the way I felt about George but Bill is a good man and I am not getting any younger.'

Noah had to admire her frankness. Hattie's relationship with the last baron was never mentioned. It was common knowledge that George had spent many a night at Laington Grace but he had never escorted Hattie to any public event. The only hint at a personal relationship was Hattie's common habit of referring to him by his given name.

Hattie watched Noah for his reaction. He was very protective of Bill. She smiled softly. She might not be in love with Bill, but he was loveable.

'People do not always marry for love,' Noah said quietly. 'Sometimes they mistake lust for love. Perhaps a genuine regard is a better basis for a marriage.'

'You have been stung!' Hattie exclaimed. 'Is that why you are determined to leave Lois?'

This was getting too personal and Noah got to his feet.

'Oh, sit down,' Hattie said impatiently. 'I love Lois like a daughter, although I am not that old! Her own mother went out of her mind and Lady Charlotte never took any notice of her until she was old enough to be useful. It was left to me and Sarah to give the care that was beyond George's realm.'

'Tell me about Lady Charlotte,' Noah asked, in an effort to distract her. 'The portrait in the master bedroom does not look like the kind of person who would take advantage of others.'

Hattie laughed. 'That is not Lady Charlotte. It is Agnes, George's first wife. I never met her as she died before I came here. She was the real love of George's life and he never forgot her. They were married for over twenty years and their children died in infancy. But George needed an heir and married Charlotte out of necessity. I won't say they hated each other but tolerance was the best they could manage. Charlotte only loved her son and even that was more to do with status than affection.'

'She obviously thought a great deal of you.' He waved his hand to indicate their surrounds.

Hattie laughed. 'That was spite. She knew how George and I felt about each other but did not dare to dismiss me in case he set me up nearby. Status and appearance were the only things that mattered to her. She was vain and when she developed dropsy, she banished all the mirrors. Towards the end I was the only person allowed into her rooms. She liked to look benevolent and willed Laington Grace to me, without any means of maintaining it.' Hattie shook her head. 'I don't know how she managed to put it about that I would be a comfort to George. It implied I was George's mistress already.'

Hattie's face softened. 'I was never George's mistress, you know. We married privately but I would never have been accepted as the baroness.' She looked at Noah, who was frowning. 'George was not ashamed of me. He said you could not be shamed by what other people thought.'

This conversation was illuminating. He needed to study the family tree again. He had meant to on many occasions but never got around to it. Was Hattie's marriage recorded there? It reminded him of something he had been curious about.

'No one talks about Simon Laing. I had assumed he was much older.'

It was Hattie's turn to be perplexed. 'What gave you that idea?'

Noah shook his head. 'He was George's son. I did not know about a much later marriage.'

Noah got to his feet again despite Hattie's protest. 'I will see about getting the solicitor. Thank you for being so open with me.'

Riding slowly back to the manor, Noah mulled over what he had learned.

Lois had shied away from any mention of her husband. At first, he had thought it was grief but later learned the grief was for George. From various comments, he had formed a picture of an older man who was more interested in pleasure than the needs of the estate. Lois would have been a convenient bride. He did not like the thought of Lois being married to anyone but at least he had not had to consider a young, vigorous man. Lois had an aura of innocence one did not associate with a sexually experienced woman.

He gave a bitter laugh. It was a sour grapes attitude. He ought to be wishing for Lois to find a congenial husband and raise the children she was so obviously fond of.

The only other person to show any interest in Noah was Rev Dunn, the retired vicar who was writing the Laing family history.

It was on a day when Lois and Mary were visiting friends for lunch. Before she left, Lois asked Noah to take lunch with the elderly priest. 'He enjoys a glass of port and it is one of the few things that will lure him away from those dusty old records,' Lois said with a smile.

Noah did not hear Dunn arrive and only knew of his presence when Pound asked him to collect the old man for lunch. 'The Reverend loses track of time,' Pound informed Noah. 'He would still be here at nightfall if we let him.' It was said indulgently and Pound added, 'I have put out the port.'

Noah went to introduce himself and found Rev Dunn engrossed in his work. His eyes lit up when Noah entered the room. He got unsteadily to his feet and bowed. 'Lord Laing, it is a pleasure to meet you.' Dunn was a thin, stooped old man with a thatch of white hair and ink-stained fingers. His eagerness to talk was a welcome change for Noah. He gladly agreed to help the reverend with Ernest's story.

'I have so often wondered what happened to him,' Dunn said as they sat down to lunch. 'I never met him as I only came to Stapleton a decade ago. What I know of Ernest is from my talks with the late baron. He tried to find his brother for years without success. I wish he could have known that you have arrived.'

Noah remembered the earliest of the letters Lois had given him to read. George had obviously shared his endeavours with Dunn so there was no need to mention them.

'Where do you want me to start?'

'From Ernest's arrival in Australia.' The old man chuckled. 'Did he stay with Mrs Mitchell? I ask for accuracy, not gossip. The history will not be made public and there are very few people still alive who knew of their elopement.'

'Gramp would not mind. He was totally unrepentant and lived happily with my grandmother for nearly forty years.' Noah did not think it necessary to say they had never married. That was too private. Gramp had kept it to himself until the very end and Noah did not think it was anyone else's business.

When it came to gathering information, Dunn was very tenacious. Any attempt by Noah to diverge from his recital was quashed. But Noah was always happy to talk about Gramp. He had been such an endearing and interesting character. Noah was happy to share what he knew of Gramp's early years in Australia.

Initially, Ernest had received money from his father but soon found employment. His early years travelling with his parents had secured him a job with a newly built theatre in Sydney. He had stayed there until his father died and he cut himself off from everything to do with England.

'After that, he travelled, taking any employment that offered. It might be tutoring or helping to build a barn. He could turn his hand to pretty much anything.'

'Did he still gamble?' Dunn asked.

'To the end,' Noah replied with a smile. 'He always carried a pair of dice that he would roll between his fingers when he was thinking. Towards the end, when there was no one to play with, he would play one hand against the other. When he died, the dice fell from his hand and landed on a double six.' Noah chuckled. 'He would have laughed at that. Luck was more often than not on his side. He did not care about winning and lost just as cheerfully. But he never bet more than he could afford to lose and cared little for whatever he won.'

'I assume he won enough to buy your sheep farm.'

'No. He won that in a card game. I remember him saying it was time I put down some roots. My mother was more than happy to settle in one place.' Noah paused as he remembered their first arrival at the farm. His mother had fallen in love with the beautiful scenery and set about turning the rather ramshackle house into a comfortable home. She had also fallen in love with and married David Owen.

Lost in his own thoughts, Noah did not notice Dunn scribbling notes on his table napkin. He had not realised he had been talking aloud until Dunn tutted in annoyance.

Noah asked what was wrong.

'I must get some paper. Mrs Laing is not going to be happy with this.' He shook the piece of linen. 'Do you think she will mind? It is only pencil and may wash out. After I have transferred all the information, of course.'

Noah agreed to accompany Dunn back to the archive room so he could continue his research. Surprisingly, they had both manged to eat the meal served but Noah had no idea what it was.

It was only the sound of the dressing gong that brought the session to a close.

'Will you have time to continue another day?' the old man asked tentatively. 'I know that you will be leaving soon.' He shook his head. 'Such a pity. I dislike leaving a task unfinished.' He looked at Noah sternly. 'You do realise that the story of Laington will not end there? I will not presume to ask what you intend to do about it but I had hoped there would be another chapter, with a happy ending.'

Noah saw the old man on his way and went up to change for dinner. He had meant to ask him about Simon, but his only question had been swept aside with the comment that Dunn had already dealt with that period. The tightening of his lips indicated that it had not been enjoyable.

More questions, Noah thought. It really ought not to matter to him, but it did.

Lois mattered to him.

He missed the quiet evening hours he had spent with Lois. They had not always been harmonious but even their quarrels had been meaningful. Now he only saw Lois at mealtimes where the conversation was about people he hardly knew. The coming weddings and departures did not appear to depress Lois. She was as contained as usual and supported the others when it came to making the arrangements.

Noah felt superfluous. He had taken to carrying his drawings of Lois around in his pocket. The soft rustle of the paper was a poor substitute for a physical touch or even a direct smile. He knew it was rubbing salt into his sore spirit, but he could not bear to throw it away. Castigating himself for being irrational and downright pathetic, he hoped a long, fast ride would shake some sense into his brain.

Chapter 18

Lois did not know how she would have survived the weeks leading up to the weddings if not for Mary's support. Her friend's lively nature and enthusiasm kept misery at bay, although the thought of Noah's leaving threatened to overwhelm her in quiet moments.

She treasured the moments she spent with Noah. Every smile, every casual touch was tucked away out of sight. She would have all the time in the world to recall them when he was gone. Lois had experienced many hard times and learned to keep her expression bland, but the effort had never been so hard.

As far as possible she tried to fill her mind with other things. Today she and Mary were taking Hattie to the dressmaker.

Lois was genuinely glad to be helping Hattie prepare for her wedding, but it underlined that there would be no such happy ending for her.

It was years since she had taken any interest in her appearance and found real enjoyment in ordering new clothes. Conversely, she tortured herself by pretending they were for a trousseau and chose each item with Noah in mind. It was ironic that Lady Charlotte had chosen Lois's wedding clothes with Simon in mind.

Lois had never been close to the baroness. In fact, she had not liked her very much. Lady Charlotte Laing had a dual personality. There was her public face, giving an impression of a caring leader of the community. Lois had to admit that many of her schemes were beneficial, but once tabled the idea had to be accomplished with little effort from the baroness.

At home, Lady Laing had been dictatorial and ungrateful for any service she received. She had treated Lois like a servant or, at best, a poor relation who should be grateful to be housed and fed and ought to repay that benefit with uncomplaining service.

Lois had not minded. She really enjoyed making life easier or more pleasant for those around her. George had praised her, in private, which was all Lois really cared about.

She had not been blind to the animosity that simmered below the surface of George and Charlotte's marriage. They were polite in public but otherwise went their own ways.

Their routine was firmly established until Lady Charlotte was afflicted with a disease that made her lethargic and bloated her body until she could barely move. The loss of her beauty made her shun company and turned her disdain into spite and jealousy. Hattie, the person she relied upon, was insulted and criticised. No one else would have tolerated such treatment. Everyone was surprised when she left Laington Grace to her maid, with a sting in the tail by implying Hattie was George's mistress.

The only person who had mourned her passing was her son, Simon. Her wish for Simon to marry Lois was based on practicality. Lois would continue to help George run the estate and not complain when Simon's interest turned to other women, a trait she actively encouraged. She did not want Lois to replace her in Simon's affections.

Lois was never quite sure how eager Simon was on his own behalf. They had known each other for years and, at first, Lois had given her child's heart to the golden boy who epitomised every storybook hero. She had been happy to take on the tasks he disliked and came to revel in the time it allowed her to spend with George.

Learning how Laington Manor and the wider estate functioned suited her desire for stability and orderliness. Gradually, pleasing George had become paramount. Her hero-worship had dimmed over time as she became aware that he was far from perfect. She could not remember when the idea of them marrying was first mentioned. It was not distasteful and had many advantages. She would get to stay at Laington and it was nice to have a handsome escort to social events. Without being vain, Lois knew she was quite pretty and there was an added fillip when Simon resented other men paying her attention.

If it had not been for the accident, Lois believed they would have had a reasonable marriage.

Seeing how Mary loved her husband brought home to Lois that 'reasonable' would never have been quite enough.

She could not help daydreaming of how it would be if she could marry Noah. Even the thought of intimacy no longer seemed something to be dreaded. The kiss had swept her away and the slightest brush of his hand set her nerves tingling. But it was not to be and Lois tried hard not to dream too often.

Mary stayed until the day before they were due to go to Bristol for Fred's wedding. Noah joined Lois in the hall to say farewell.

As Nanny carried baby Alex down the stairs, Lois ran forward and asked for one last cuddle. It stole Noah's breath when Lois bent to kiss the baby's head. There were tears in her eyes as she reluctantly handed Alex back to his nurse. Noah had to fight the urge to take her into his arms. It was not passion or even desire. It was a yearning for the child to be hers and for them both to be his.

Lois's tears fell as she hugged Mary. Mary patted her back and whispered before gently freeing herself. The look she threw at Noah was enough to make him step back and content himself with a nod of farewell. He remained on the doorstep until the carriage pulled away and when he turned, Lois was already halfway up the stairs. He resisted the urge to follow her. The way she had been avoiding him of late did not suggest she would welcome his comfort now.

Noah went through the rear of the house to the stables. Perhaps a gallop over the fields would clear the image of Lois from his mind. He was vaguely aware that the carriage had been rolled out and of Tommy leading the carriage horses in from the paddock, but he was in no mood for conversation.

Once clear of the buildings, Noah set Juno into a gallop. He had always enjoyed riding. The feeling of power mixed with humility put things into perspective. Gramp had told him never to assume he was in command of a horse. The animal was much more powerful than a man. It took a mutual respect and trust for it to respond to the slightest touch.

He let Juno choose their route, his mind still focused on that strange sensation at the sight of Lois and the baby. He had never felt anything like it. Certainly not with his own wife or daughter.

He had initially desired Clara. He'd been twenty, healthy and ripe for romance. She had been a vivacious eighteen-year-old red-head with an alluring figure and enticing smile. He had felt smug at cutting out her other admirers. They had married in haste after succumbing to temptation. The infatuation of youth had quickly faded. Away from the glitter of ballrooms, Clara became bored and petulant when Noah refused to return to a live of idle gaiety in Adelaide.

Clara had had a hard pregnancy. Noah was on the point of taking her back to her mother when Gramp had a heart attack. One delay had led to another until it was too late for her to travel.

He had never stopped feeling guilty for failing her. When she died giving birth, he had felt he owed it to her to ensure the survival of her child. He had found an Aboriginal woman to nurse the baby and arranged a hasty funeral for Clara. There had been no time to mourn his wife, and no heartbreak when he left his daughter in the care of her maternal aunt.

Now his heart felt heavy with regret for what might have been.

Noah slowed Juno to a walk. It was not fair to push her beyond her limits. They had come a long way without him realising. He dismounted and loosened the girth, allowing Juno to amble along behind him on a long rein.

He was still lost in thought when he heard someone call his name.

'Ho, there, Laing!'

Noah was surprised at the eagerness in John Pritchard's voice. They had met on frequent occasions but there had always been a coolness on John's part. Which Noah could understand. John obviously had a high regard, even love, for Lois and probably saw Noah as a rival. Now it was known that he would be leaving, the man felt able to greet him in a friendly manner.

The assumption was confirmed when John pulled up close. 'All set for the off?' he said cheerfully.

Noah chose to misunderstand. 'Yes. We leave for Bristol in the morning.'

John frowned. 'Oh. The Norton weddings. Are you keeping out of the way of all the fuss?'

'Yes,' Noah replied shortly. *But not for the reasons you think*, he muttered under his breath. He rather liked the other man but at this moment would prefer not to discuss weddings with him. 'You will be glad to see the back of me.'

'That's plain speaking,' John said in surprise, 'but you are right. I thought history was going to repeat itself and Lois would marry you.'

'You want her yourself.'

John got down and let his horse amble over to where Juno was grazing. 'I would marry her tomorrow if she would have me but I was resigned to the fact that Lois would never marry again.'

'She loved her husband so much?' It was a very intrusive question but Noah could not help asking it.

'She idolised him.' John looked away and firmed his lips as though considering what to say. When he turned back to Noah he asked, 'Is that what has been holding you back?'

It flashed through Noah's mind that perhaps the man was right and impulsively replied, 'I have no wish to step into a dead man's shoes.'

'Simon was my friend,' John said quietly. 'That never changed but Simon did after the accident.'

Noah felt a rush of anger. 'Did he mistreat her? Was he unfaithful?'

'I won't answer that. As I said, Simon was my friend.' Without a word of farewell John jumped onto his horse and rode away.

Noah watched him go, trying to unravel the hidden message. So many things had fallen into place recently. Lois had married her idol but never willingly spoke of him. Other people also avoided mentioning him. Mary had spoken of him disapprovingly and even Rev Dunn had refused to talk about him. Hattie had mentioned him only in connection to his selfish mother.

Juno had drawn close and huffed gently at Noah's neck. He patted her and looked into her eyes with a smile. 'I suspect you could tell me a thing or two, my friend, but I need to find out for myself.' He adjusted the saddle and rode back to the manor deep in thought.

Juno quickened her pace as they neared the stable and Farmer came out to meet them. Noah dismounted and handed over the reins. 'She is a fine animal. One I would be proud to own,' Noah told him. 'We have had a gallop and she needs a good rub down.'

Farmer nodded. 'I'll see to it but you never get her lathered up. A good horse can be ruined with bad handling.' He looked as though he wanted to add more but thought better of it. With a nod to Noah, he led Juno into the stable.

When Noah entered the house, Pound informed him that Mrs Laing had gone into town.

Noah was quite relieved. He had things to do before he spoke to Lois again. He went straight up to the gallery. There must be a portrait of Simon somewhere. He found it at the far end, beyond the point of Lois's tour.

It was a conventional portrait of the young heir to a title seated on Ja fine horse. Noah was relieved that he did not recognise himself in the subject. They shared some of the same family features but Noah hoped he had never worn that expression.

Noah could draw and understood that this was not a representation of a single moment. A portrait took time and was made up of numerous sketches and perhaps a few sittings. It was very well done by an accomplished artist.

The eyes were cold rather than interested. The lips smirked rather than smiled. The proud tilt of his head spoke of arrogance. At first glance, Simon appeared relaxed, but the position of his hands told another story. The fingers of the left hand had been caught drumming impatiently on his thigh. The crop in his right hand lay across Jupiter's neck with the illusion of pressure.

Noah switched his attention to the horse. He could almost feel the tension of its bunched muscles. Its ears and eyes held a wariness that Noah would not have trusted.

The portrait was cleverly done. Only someone who knew Simon intimately would spot all the clues. Others would just see the traits they were familiar with.

Noah disliked the man intensely.

He turned away and went to the archive room. He spread out the family tree and studied the dates.

The first thing he spotted was the date of George's marriage to Hattie. He had to smile as he remembered Hattie saying George had not been ashamed of her. Their marriage had taken place a bare two months after Lady Charlotte's death.

George's first marriage had lasted for nearly twenty years. A son and daughter had died in infancy. Noah did some mental arithmetic and worked out that George had not married Charlotte until he was in his fifties. Simon had been born less than two years later.

The dates of Simon's marriage and death were also less than two years apart.

That took Noah by surprise. Lois had been a widow for nearly six years! He had assumed Simon's death to be much more recent.

He tried to recall the details of George's earlier letters. When had they changed from invitations for Ernest to return home to hinting, then confirming, that Noah was his heir? He would have to wait for answers as the dressing gong had just sounded.

Chapter 19

Lois was glad she had arranged to take Hattie into town to collect their dresses for Fred and Ruby's wedding. It meant she had to put on a brave face, and it kept her away from Noah.

The way he had looked when he saw her saying goodbye to baby Alex broke her heart. It was a look of such longing he must have been reminded of the little daughter he had left behind in Australia. She loved Alex and could not imagine how hard it would be to leave one's own child.

Hattie's enthusiasm for their errand was infectious and distracted Lois from her gloomy thoughts.

Hattie had always loved new clothes. Her years as a maid, handling beautiful clothes every day while she was dressed in a drab maid's uniform, had been a trial for her.

Lady Charlotte had always kept up with the latest fashion, discarding little-worn garments with instructions to get rid of them. Hattie had done just that. She had an arrangement with a local dressmaker who purchased the dresses and sent them to contacts in distant parts of the country so there was no chance of the baroness meeting anyone wearing one of her cast-offs. Hattie had saved the proceeds and spent most of the money on bright and ornate gowns until George died. Then she had taken to wearing black all the time, just as an acknowledged widow would have done.

The only people who knew of Hattie and George's marriage were Rev Dunn, who had performed the ceremony with Lois and Sarah as witnesses. Hattie had not even told her twin sister, who could not be trusted to keep the news to herself.

Now Hattie was ready to make a new start. She had ordered a completely new wardrobe for her life in Australia, choosing practical styles and materials in colours befitting a woman of mature years. She would appear in Bristol as Bill's intended bride and, laughing, said she planned to outshine Ruby.

The expedition nicely filled the afternoon and Lois did not return to the manor until it was almost time to change for dinner.

When Noah came down for dinner, he asked Lois to spare him a moment. She could not refuse and reluctantly joined him in the main office.

'I have instructed Hemmings to pay Bill for all the hours he has put in working with the shepherd and other labourers. I remembered something Hattie said about Bill not wanting to live on her annuity. I ought to have thought of it before. I have been happy to finance Bill, but Hattie said a man had to have his pride.'

'I ought to have thought of it too,' Lois replied happily. She was so relieved Noah had not opened a personal subject, she would have agreed to almost any suggestion. 'I hope you made it generous.'

'Not too generous,' Noah said. 'That would look like charity and erode Bill's pride in a different way.'

There was short pause which Lois rushed to fill. 'I am amazed at the change in Bill recently. He is no longer shy and makes far fewer mistakes in his speech and manners.'

'That is the pride I spoke of. He is free of duress and worry about his brother and able to reveal his true nature. I believe the and Hattie will be very happy.' Noah added, tentatively, 'Hattie told me she had been married to George.'

Lois laughed. 'You are honoured. That was their big secret. It appealed to their sense of humour, making no effort to hide a relationship some thought dishonourable.'

Noah wondered how dishonourable it would have been in any case. Both were free of other commitments and, given George's advanced age and hints of ill-health, he suspected it had been more a close companionship than a passionate affair.

The unwelcome thought of Lois in a passionate relationship with a young man soured Noah's mood and he suggested they go through to the dining room.

Lois agreed with a heavy heart. Now he had settled the matter of his friend's pride, Noah could not wait to get away from her.

Bill almost pounced on them when they entered the dining room. 'Hemmings has given me a wodge of money. He said it was my back wages!'

Noah laughed. 'Yes. We are sorry you have not been receiving them regularly.'

'Aw! There was no need. I owe you enough already.'

Lois touched his arm. 'It was not a personal gift. The estate has benefitted from your talents and hard work. We pay our dues.'

Bill seemed to grow an extra few inches, but his reply was typical. 'I had nothing else to do.'

'I have been living here rent free, too,' Fred added. 'I think I understand your helping Bill, but you have no reason to feel responsible for me.'

'Laington does not take payment from guests,' Lois assured him and signalled the footman to serve the first course.

Lois did not enjoy the meal. She ate very little and had to force that down past the lump in her throat. She was aware that Noah was watching her but avoided meeting his eyes.

Bill glanced between them, aware of the tension, and kindly kept Fred talking about the arrangements Mrs Drayton had been making for a grand wedding reception.

Lois wished she could back out of attending but she really wanted to meet Ruby, who would be Hattie's companion on the voyage and would be a close neighbour when they arrived. She had no fears of Hattie settling into her new home, but her life would be more pleasant if she had a friendly relationship with Fred's bride.

As soon as the meal was over, Lois said she was very tired and would retire early. Noah escorted her to the door and murmured, 'Are you feeling unwell?'

'Just tired,' she replied. 'The next few days will be busy and I need an early night. Excuse me.' Lois felt his eyes like a touch on her back as she hurried up the stairs with more energy than would be expected of someone who claimed to be very tired.

Noah watched her go with a heavy heart. He was worried. Lois was good at hiding her feelings, but she had been very pale. Even the dusky pink of her gown had failed to reflect any colour into her cheeks. He did not want to rejoin the happy brothers and went up to his room.

As he passed the study, Noah remembered he still had the file of George's letters. Some of the comments made today prompted him to read through them again.

Now, knowing the date of his son's death, George's earlier letters made much more sense. John had spoken of a change in Simon after the accident. Farmer had hinted that someone had mistreated a horse. Simon's portrait had revealed much more. The man showed impatience and Jupiter had been tense.

Noah concluded that Jupiter had thrown him. The dates did not match a fatal accident, but Simon had died less than two years later.

As he returned the file to the case, Noah noticed another folder bearing Ernest's name. The letters it contained were all from Ernest, written to George while they were growing up. Some of the comments were obscure, answers to questions Noah surmised George had asked in his letters, of which there were no copies. In the earliest letters, Ernest had complained about the school routine. Later, it was about his exploits as a young man-about-town. They had continued for a while after Ernest went to Australia, telling George things that Noah already knew. Gramp had never been reluctant to talk about his life in the colony. It was only the English years he had kept silent about until he was dying.

Noah also knew why the letters stopped. After his father died, Ernest had been ordered home to assume his duties as heir. He had replied in blunt terms and thereafter, he had taken steps to conceal his movements.

Had they been entirely successful, Noah would not be sitting here now.

With a sigh, he replaced the folder and left it on the desk ready to return to Lois and went to bed. Surprisingly, sleep claimed him within moments.

Chapter 20

By the next morning, Lois had her emotions back under control.

Lying in bed last night, she had tried to put things into perspective. It was that look on Noah's face that had disturbed her so much. She could understand his longing for his child. It did him credit and she was determined to let him go without any hint of how she felt. It would be hard but she was well practiced at hiding her feelings.

They met at breakfast, shared a carriage to the train with Hattie and Fred with Bill riding beside the driver. She and Hattie completed the journey in a ladies-only compartment and once in Bristol, there were too many people to meet for much introspection.

Mr Drayton met them at the station and, after the introductions, sent Lois and Hattie on to his house in the carriage. He explained briefly that the men would be spending the night in a hotel. 'My wife will not risk any ill-omens should Fred catch sight of Ruby before the ceremony tomorrow. I will escort them there now and see you later.'

Lois thought it a rather odd way of doing things. She and Hattie were to turn up on a strange woman's doorstep without any introduction!

She need not have worried. Mrs Drayton had been hovering at the window and rushed out to greet them on the doorstep.

'It is so good of you to come,' she said, holding on to Lois's hand. 'Bill told us how you run a great house and I am relying on you to let me know if I have forgotten anything.'

A rotund man standing behind her said, 'You get the ladies inside, Beryl, while I see to their bags.'

'Oh, yes, yes. Thank you, Joe.' She turned to Hattie. 'I have not said hello to you yet. I am so excited. Please come in, both of you.'

'You haven't told them who I am either,' the man commented quietly as they moved passed him. He lowered his voice while Mrs Drayton was greeting Hattie. 'I'm Joe, Beryl's brother.

Pleased to meet you. I've been roped in to act as butler for the big day.'

Lois was hard put not to laugh. Joe could do with a few lessons from Pound. A butler would never appear in his shirt sleeves and braces!

That set the tone of the visit. The house might be grand, but the occupants were down-to-earth people.

Lois liked the Draytons. She warmed to Mrs Drayton straight away. She was so welcoming and eager to please, one could forgive her fussing.

Dinner that evening was to be a quiet affair. Even so, Mrs Drayton, 'Please call me Beryl,' asked Lois to check the table and took her straight to the dining room. 'I was not sure where everyone should sit,' she confessed. 'I am still not used to all this.' She waved her hand around. 'I don't know how I will manage without Ruby.'

The table was not over large but set with an array of silver and glassware. 'Don't worry,' Lois reassured her hostess. 'It is just a family dinner so you and Mr Drayton will take your usual seats and let the others choose for themselves.' Lois looked around the richly furnished room. 'Is this where you will hold the wedding breakfast?'

'Oh, no. That is being held at the Royal Hotel. They will arrange everything,' Beryl said with a sigh of relief.

'There you are, Mum,' said Ruby from the doorway. She smiled at Lois. 'Hello to you too, Mrs Laing. As you may have guessed, I am Ruby. I have shown Hattie up to her room and wondered where you had got to.'

Ruby was tall, dark and rather plain until she smiled. Lois liked her open friendliness and said, 'Please call me Lois.'

'Mum, will you take Lois upstairs while I check on the refreshments?'

Beryl suddenly remembered her duties as hostess. 'Oh, yes. You are still wearing your hat and gloves. Please come with me.'

Going up the stairs, Beryl continued talking about her lack of entertaining skills. 'I am still not used to all this grandeur. In Whitby my friends and I would sit around the kitchen table, drinking tea and chatting about our families. If they wanted to take off their coats they did so. We only kept one maid and I did all the cooking.' She sighed. 'I must be a great disappointment to William. He has risen in the world and I feel I am letting him down.'

Lois made soothing noises. She could understand Beryl's insecurities. Fred had told her about Mr Drayton's rise from small-time fisherman to owner of a growing fleet. Beryl was the kind of woman who was happiest taking care of her family in rather basic conditions.

'The best thing is not to worry,' Lois advised her. 'Your welcome is more important and you made me feel comfortable straight away.'

The four women had finished their light lunch and were getting to know each other when the men returned. Fred and Bill's descriptions had been almost perfect. When Mr Drayton returned, she was able to see past his dour appearance to the proud and loving father who was about to see his daughter depart for the far side of the world.

Mr Drayton immediately and unselfconsciously kissed his wife's cheek. Fred drew Ruby to the far side of the room for a more discreet kiss. Bill patted Hattie's shoulder and winked.

Lois dared not look at Noah in case he thought she was begging for a token of affection.

Mr Drayton explained their delay in returning. 'We had a bite at the hotel.' He smiled at his wife. 'I was sure you would take care of the ladies.' He did not sound or act like a man who was disappointed in his wife.

The conversation became general, mostly about the coming wedding. Lois was relieved to hear that Beryl would have plenty of support. Her elder daughter was to be Ruby's matron of honour and would be spending the night here. Other family members, who had travelled down from Yorkshire, would be staying at the same hotel as Fred.

'I hope they will not keep him in the bar all night,' Ruby said firmly. 'I know what they are like when they all get together. I will not make my vows if you are drunk,' she told Fred.

Fred protested that he knew his limits and never got drunk. Everyone laughed when Bill admitted that he could get drunk on very little and Hattie said she hoped he would remember his promise.

The relaxed atmosphere carried them through the rest of the day.

Fred had described Ruby as an angel of patience, which was underlined in her calm way of dealing with her mother's insecurities.

'I was beginning to worry that this wedding would never take place,' Beryl confided. 'I feared Ruby would be too old to have children before Fred was able to marry her.' She smiled softly. 'Children are so precious.'

Lois bent her head to hide a rush of scalding tears.

Beryl touched her hand. 'Oh, you poor dear girl. Now I have upset you. I am so sorry. You are very young to be a widow. Did your husband die suddenly?'

Lois wiped away her tears. Beryl had not meant to be insensitive and was not being nosey. 'He had been suffering for a long time,' Lois said quietly. 'It was almost a relief when he died.' She looked into the kindly woman's eyes. 'That must make me sound an awful person.'

'Not at all. There can be nothing worse than seeing a loved one suffer.'

From the far side of the room, Noah saw Lois wiping her tears. Fearing Mrs Drayton's ineptitude had upset her, his instinct was to go to her rescue. He took one step in their direction but Mrs Drayton gave him a warning look and a slight shake of her head. He stayed where he was but kept checking that Lois was alright.

Lois had never shared how she felt about Simon, even with her closest friends. Admitting it to a virtual stranger seemed to lift the burden of guilt. She smiled at Beryl.

'Thank you for being so understanding. I did not have a happy marriage. I wished I had not married Simon, but I never wished him dead. I am glad I have been able to talk to someone about it. I wish you were my mother.'

Ruby had approached in time to hear Lois's final words and said, 'She is the best mum in the world. I think you should adopt her.'

The groups reshuffled and Lois was drawn into conversation with Mr Drayton, and she heard of another side to Ruby's character. He had looked across the room at his daughter and shaken his head. 'Fred is going to have his hands full. Ruby is not as docile as she appears. She will promise to obey but she has a will of her own. Sparks will fly if he tries to cosset her too much.'

The arrival of Ruby's sister, Pearl, broke up the party and the ladies all trooped up the stairs to view the wedding outfits before retiring to bed.

Next morning, Pearl banished her mother from Ruby's bedroom. She was less tolerant than her sister so it fell to Lois and Hattie to stop Beryl panicking when the flowers were not delivered on the dot of nine.

The wedding was to be at eleven and the house was quickly filling with aunts, uncles and cousins. The Drayton men were all tall and dark, with gruff voices and loud comments on the grand house. Their womenfolk were more interested in updating Beryl on family news. They were all unashamedly working people. Happy with their lives and unenvious of William Drayton's rise in the world.

Beryl's side of the family was limited to her brother, Joe, who was now suitably dressed as a butler but had yet to assume a suitable manner. He came in for much ribbing which he took in good part, saying the curtain had not gone up yet. The enigmatic statement was explained by Ruby's brother, Jasper.

He looked more like his mother and was less exuberant than the rest of the males present. 'Uncle Joe is an actor,' Jasper told Lois after he had been introduced. 'Mum would be terrified of a real butler. She finds it hard enough to cope with extra maids.'

Lois liked the young man who was about her own age. He stayed close to Lois and took it upon himself to introduce her to the various family members. There were all friendly but there were too many for Lois to remember their names and to whom they were married.

It was soon time to leave for the church. A line of carriages filled the street and there was much jostling for seats. Jasper found Lois a seat with some of the younger relations. 'We have been decorating Ruby's carriage,' one of the girls remarked. 'The boys tie on the pots and pans after the ceremony. I hope Auntie Beryl does not mind the nice things being bumped along the road.'

Lois could not help remembering her own wedding. There had been no horseplay or jollity. Everyone except her was wearing black in mourning for the recently deceased baroness. George had overruled Simon's suggestion that Lois ought to be wearing black as well. 'Not on her wedding day,' George had declared. 'You must wait until Lois is actually your wife before you give the orders.'

It had not gone down well and set the tone for what was to follow.

Fred and Ruby's wedding day was a whirl of activity and laughter. Although the couple had wanted a quiet wedding, they had not taken into account the lively nature of Ruby's family. They were uninhibited, without airs and graces. This was a happy occasion and they enjoyed it to the full.

Lois had attended many weddings but never anything like this. She was one of the few unrelated guests but accepted without question and embraced by people whose names she could not remember. For a few hours she forgot her own sorrows.

There were a number of very young guests, children of Ruby's friends and young cousins. They were not kept apart as would have happened in a higher society. Small children were passed around for cuddles while the slightly older cajoled senior members into joining games of tag.

When the dancing began it touched Lois's heart to see children being whirled around in their parents' arms.

Out of breath from dancing a lively polka, Lois flopped into a seat beside Hattie. 'Are you enjoying yourself?' she asked, fanning her heated cheeks.

'It reminds me of Harvest Home parties when I was a girl,' Hattie replied with a reminicient smile. 'I had almost forgotten what it was like to be part of a family.'

Hattie seldom spoke of her childhood as a member of a large, working-class family. When they reached working age, her brothers and sisters had been dispersed far and wide. They were not very literate and even the penny post could not keep them in close touch. At the age of twelve, Hattie and her twin sister, Betty, had been forced into the formal setting of an aristocratic household. Charlotte Laing did not consider her staff beyond expecting excellent service. It had never occurred to her to arrange entertainments for them.

George had been more appreciative but his thanks had usually been of a monetary kind.

With no close example to follow, it was years before Lois understood what was missing from her life and theirs. It was only when she became involved with the wider community that she has seen pleasure did not have to rely on fancy clothes and lavish entertainments. The company of loving people could turn a simple meeting into an occasion of joy.

Lois put aside the gloomy memories and patted her friend's hand. 'With Ruby and Fred close by you will have the start of a family again.'

Lois had spoken to comfort, but it also implied that Hattie would not have children of her own. The gloomy thoughts were gaining ground again and Lois got to her feet. She was not sure what to do next, only that she was in danger of dwelling on her own sadness.

Noah had also been absorbed into the boisterous company. The atmosphere was not new to him. Ernest had been gregarious and made friends wherever he went, carrying Noah and his mother along with him. He had no regard for class or wealth and treated everyone as equals. Noah had celebrated finds in a goldfield and Christmas in a lumber camp. Throughout it all, Ernest had remained a true gentleman and taught Noah how to behave in any situation. 'Watch and learn,' had been Gramp's advice. 'You will see how to fit in.'

Noah had spent much of his time watching Lois. She seemed to be enjoying herself although, yesterday, he had caught her wiping tears from her eyes while talking to Mrs Drayton. When he had moved towards them, Beryl had given a tiny shake of her head. Noah knew that look. His mother wore it when his company would not be welcome. 'Woman's business,' it announced.

Today Lois had shed her reserve and joined in the activities with every sign of enthusiasm. The dress she had chosen was of some material that shimmered like the tail of a peacock. It matched the sparkle in her eyes as she was twirled around by one or other of the Drayton men. He had not asked her to dance but did not think it was obvious as he had been fully occupied partnering other ladies.

He became aware of a general stir as everyone turned towards the door. He had been too busy to miss the bridal pair, who now stood in the doorway dressed for departure.

Joe Drayton gave a booming call for attention as maids circulated with trays of glasses. 'Don't drink it yet,' he ordered. 'William wants to say a few words.'

'Make sure it is only a few, lad,' called an elderly man, raising laughter all round.

William placed one arm around his wife and the other round Ruby. 'I am not going to make a speech.'

'Thank goodness for that,' someone else quipped.

William waited for the laughter to subside before he continued. 'I just want you all to raise your glasses and wish Ruby and Fred a marriage as happy as ours has been.' He hugged Beryl closer. 'To Fred, my new son, and Ruby, a jewel as precious as her name.'

'Ruby and Fred!' everyone chorused, followed by cheers and a rush to accompany the couple out to the waiting carriage. It had been festooned with the traditional pots and pans and ribbons. Everyone seemed to have a flower or two, which they hurled into the carriage. Ruby stood up and surveyed the throng. Several young ladies were vying for the best position to catch her bouquet, but Ruby lobbed it expertly over their heads to Hattie.

That was not the end of the celebrations. Everyone migrated back to the Draytons' home and continued partying until they left in ones and twos to bed down the sleepy children. The younger men departed for a local tavern and their elders settled down to rehash the day.

William Drayton invited Noah and Bill into his den. 'You won't want to hear about every family wedding in the last fifty years,' he commented. 'I have been wanting a private word with you,' he said to Bill when they were comfortably seated. 'I like your Hattie. It relieves my mind that Ruby will have a female companion on the journey. They seem to be getting on well.'

He turned to Noah. 'How close will they be living?'

'That depends on Fred getting the job I will recommend him for. I have shares in a river steamer on the Murray. Their base is ten or twelve miles downstream. There will be other opportunities if that does not work out, but I cannot see Fred being happy if it has nothing to do with boats.'

William laughed. 'I can understand that. I am not so involved in the sailing or boat building now, but shipping is in my blood.'

Bill nudged Noah. 'Do you get sick on a river boat?'

Noah groaned. 'I wish you would forget about that. I don't want half the population of Australia to know that I am a disgrace to my name!'

Joe poked his head around the door to say the last of the guests were leaving. 'Beryl says she can make up beds for Bill and Noah.'

Bill looked hopeful, but Noah said they would not put her to the trouble and would return to their hotel.

Lois had already retired to bed. With the thinning company, her thoughts had turned inward again and she did not want to spoil the evening with a gloomy face.

Chapter 21

Lois and Hattie had breakfasted with Beryl next morning. William Drayton had left earlier and would collect Noah and Bill in time to catch their train back to Laington.

'It will feel strange for it to be just me and William,' Beryl said. 'It will be just like old times if it was not for the maids and this big house of course. I was quite happy in our cottage. I managed everything, shopping and cooking. Now I have to tell other people to do things and never know if they do it properly. It worries me but the people William mixes with now would think it very odd if I did the housework myself.'

'You worry too much about what other people think,' Lois told her.

'Yes,' Hattie agreed. 'Be yourself and let them lump it! That's what I did.'

'But it might affect William's business. He has worked so hard to get where he is now.'

'Unless you do something really outrageous, no one will take much notice.'

'I was talking to one of your sisters-in-law yesterday,' Hattie added. 'Sorry, I can't remember her name. She said you were the mainstay of their community in Whitby and they miss you.'

Beryl nodded. 'It was different there. There was always someone in need of help and I knew them all. Everyone was the same. We just helped each other.'

'There must be people in Bristol who would appreciate your help.'

'But I don't know them.' Beryl was nearly crying. 'I can't just, well, I just can't.'

Lois patted her hand. 'Your vicar seemed very nice,' she said gently. 'Go and thank him for a lovely service. Tell him you have time on your hands and he will be glad to find you something useful to do.'

'I could do that,' Beryl agreed eagerly. 'It is all the social rules I don't understand.'

Hattie thought for a moment before suggesting, 'You need someone who knows what's what to guide you. Perhaps you could give my housekeeper a trial. She will need a new post when I leave.'

Beryl's look of horror made Lois laugh. 'That might just be the thing. Molly is a quiet, kind woman. She was trained at the manner but was not considered strict enough to be appointed housekeeper there. She won't try to take over your role, just see to all the day-to-day tasks.'

Hattie nodded. 'Lois is right. Molly is very understanding and won't get upset if you want to cook for William or do some of the lighter housework. You can't really hanker to do the washing and scrub floors!'

Beryl laughed. 'I have not had to do that for years!'

They were still laughing when the men arrived.

When it was time for them to leave, William drew Lois to one side. 'Thank you for coming. It has made a world of difference to Beryl. She is almost back to her true self.' He looked across to where his wife was hugging Hattie. 'I was beginning to get worried.'

'I think Beryl is a little bit shy, overwhelmed and anxious not to let you down.'

'She could never do that,' William replied stanchly. 'I wanted to give her all the things I could not afford before not realising that they were weighing her down. I am grateful to you for encouraging her.'

Impulsively, Lois gave him a quick hug and joined Beryl near the door. 'Thank you for a lovely stay. I hope you take to Molly and find your way around the new community.' She kissed Beryl's cheek and went out to the waiting carriage.

When Noah helped her in, the touch of his hand made her tremble and she missed the step. Next moment she was held firmly in his arms with her head resting against his chest. Lois wanted to stay there forever but, from inside the carriage, Hattie called, 'Whoops a daisy,' breaking the moment.

Noah saw Lois safely settled before climbing in to sit beside Bill on the opposite seat. They all leant forward to wave goodbye before settling back for the short ride to the railway station.

'That was a very pleasant visit,' Noah remarked. 'I hardly recognised Mrs Drayton from my first visit a month ago.'

'We have sorted that,' Hattie said proudly and went on to explain. 'She is a home body who had been taken away from the life she knew. It sapped her confidence and made her look helpless.'

Noah stifled a groan. How many more times was he to be reminded that a woman could be destroyed if uprooted from all that is familiar. Lost in his thoughts, he did not hear Hattie giving more details to Bill.

'Beryl likes to cook, which will please Molly, if she is taken on. She has tried to teach me but all the cooking talent in my family went to Betty.' She looked across at Bill. 'You will have to put up with my poor efforts.'

'I'm not fussy, as long as there is plenty of it!' Bill said, patting his stomach.

Lois was relieved that she did not need to join in the banter. She was trying to hold on to the feeling of being in Noah's arms. She had no idea how long the embrace had lasted but it had been heaven. She was vaguely aware of her other companions laughing although she had lost track of the topic. Fortunately, they had arrived at the station and were soon caught up in the bustle of finding seats. The train was quite full and private conversation was out of the question.

The Laington carriage was waiting for them at the Halt. They would drop Hattie off first, before going on to the manor.

As Lois approached the carriage, she was surprised to see a strange man with two large bags speaking to Farmer and the crossing keeper. The Halt was not a public station and she wondered what he was doing there.

'Why, there is Mr Harris! I was not expecting him until tomorrow!' Noah exclaimed and walked quickly ahead.

Beside her, Hattie said, 'I asked Noah's advice about what I want to do with Laington Grace. He said he would get your solicitor to call.'

Noah performed the introductions. 'Please excuse my early arrival, Mrs Laing. Given the complexity of this business and with time of the essence, I thought we should give it as much time as possible.'

Lois was slightly confused. Hattie had told her what she planned and it had not sounded very difficult. Years of practice had her putting irrelevant thoughts aside, and she smiled reassuringly. 'It is no inconvenience, Mr Harris. You are very welcome.' She turned to consult Hattie. 'Do you still want to go home straight away?'

Hattie shook her head. 'If Mr Harris does not mind, I would like to hear what he advises and make a decision tomorrow.'

It had started to rain so the bags were quickly loaded and they piled into the carriage for the short journey to the manor. Bill, as usual, took his preferred place on the box with Farmer. On arrival, Lois was too busy giving instructions for refreshments and Mr Harris's accommodation to hear Noah ask him quietly, not to mention the transfer of the Laington estate until he had prepared Lois.

Hattie had gone straight through to the small room always kept prepared for the comfort of lady visitors, so Lois went up to her own room to attend to urgent needs. She could trust Pound to offer similar facilities to the newcomer.

Lois removed her outdoor clothes and as she tidied her hair, an earlier thought returned. Hattie was putting her affairs in order and Lois hoped the solicitor would remind Noah that he had things to settle too. She also needed to talk to Mr Harris about her own situation. She had no idea where she would stand if Noah decided to sell the estate. George's will had given her a home for life, but would it still stand if there was a new owner?

She would not be destitute. Lady Charlotte had left her personal fortune to Simon, and it had passed to Lois on his death. It included a house in London which was at present rented out. Lois had never seen it but it would offer a complete change of scenery when or if she needed to leave Laington.

Lois was well practiced at putting her own needs aside and left the room to attend to her duties as mistress of the house.

Refreshments were served in the drawing room. Old Mr Harris had always been treated as a friend rather than an agent and Lois thought George would want her to offer the same courtesy to the younger man.

'This is very pleasant,' Mr Harris said, sitting comfortably with a cup of tea and a plate of sandwiches on a table by his side. 'My father told me about Laington but this is much grander than I expected.' He gazed around, mentally tallying the value of its contents.

'It almost knocked me over when I first arrived,' Bill commented. 'It has been very kind of Lois to have me here, but it is not the way I would want to go on forever.' He smiled sheepishly at Lois. 'Sorry if that sounds ungrateful.'

'Not at all.' Lois knew how nervous Bill had been of doing something wrong and causing offence.

Bill continued. 'I'm not saying I would want to go back to living in two rooms and not knowing if we would eat again tomorrow, but all this' – he waved his hands – 'who needs special rooms for different things? My mam did the cooking and washing in the kitchen and taught us our letters at the table after the dishes were cleared. And there are all the things that never get used.' He stopped suddenly and looked at the faces of the people around him. 'Sorry,' he muttered. 'I am being rude. But I don't understand why.'

'It is heritage,' Mr Harris said, scandalised. 'The family goes back hundreds of years.'

Bill shrugged. 'I suppose mine must have as well. But its people who matter, not the bits and pieces they have collected.'

Hattie touched his arm. In their private conversations Bill had said even more, and she did not want him to alienate the solicitor before he had sorted out her own inheritance. 'Well, don't worry about it now, love. I want to hear what Mr Harris thinks of my little scheme.'

Lois got to her feet. 'I will leave you to talk to Mr Harris. Do you want to go home after or will you stay for dinner?'

'I think I will go home and talk things over with Bill before I sign anything.' Hattie's reply indicated that she would be taking Bill out of the way before he let any more of his deeper feelings out. She could see that Mr Harris's snooty attitude was annoying him.

Noah also got to his feet and followed Lois from the room. Before she could move away, he caught hold of her hand. 'There are things I need to discuss with you. May we go into your office?'

Lois allowed him to keep hold of her hand as they crossed the hall but put the desk between them as soon as they were alone. She rushed into speech. 'Did Hattie tell you she wants to give me Laington Grace?'

Noah recognised the comment as a diversion. Lois did not want to talk to him but was too polite to turn him down.

'Please sit down,' he said. 'I need to talk to you about this property.'

Lois had dreaded this moment. He had come to a decision at last. She sat and gripped her hands tightly together under the desk top and blanked her face.

'I asked Mr Harris to come for my benefit as well as Hattie's.' Noah looked at Lois's apparently calm expression and sighed. 'I am going to transfer ownership of Laington to you.' He held up his hand when Lois looked about to speak. 'Hear me out. I had already decided but Bill's comments underline how right it is. You love and appreciate Laington far more than I ever could. It holds your memories, not mine. My only connection is through Gramp, who had never wanted to inherit and made a new life for himself. I feel that is where my ancestry starts.'

Lois closed her eyes, trying to take in the enormity of his proposal. She had never been meant to own Laington, just to be a support to Simon. Noah's final words echoed how she felt. Somehow her life had started with George. She only had vague images of her previous home, few of them particularly pleasing. Everything she was, she owed to George, absorbing his obsession about the estate until the two were inseparable.

Lois had been quiet for so long, Noah asked, 'Are you alright?'

Lois looked up and replied tartly, 'Of course not! You can't just give Laington away. You have a daughter and it is possible you will marry again and have a son. How will they feel when they are old enough to understand that you have given away their birthright?'

'That isn't going to happen.'

'Can you see into the future? I wish I could.' Lois left her seat. 'I will not discuss this until I have spoken to Mr Harris. I do not believe it is possible. It certainly is not right.'

Noah could have detailed her by force but stood aside for her to leave the room. He raked a hand through his hair and huffed out a breath of frustration. He did not understand women. You never knew which way they would jump.

His mother had married his father knowing what a miserable sod he was in the hope of having children. She had trailed around Australia without a word of complaint to make sure her only son was well cared for. Her own wishes had been put aside until she felt her duty had been done.

Hattie was willing to give away a substantial income for the sake of Bill's pride.

Their choices had been made willingly and based on love.

Clara was the opposite. She had professed to love him but it had not been strong enough to compensate for the loss of her social standing and the lack of entertainment. When she did not get her own way, she sulked until it became a true depression and led to her death.

Even Mrs Drayton had seen her husband's rise in the world and the benefits it brought as a burden. There was no lack of love but she had not really been given a choice.

He had not expected Lois to show elation at being given the estate that was the centre of her existence. That was not her way. A quiet demur would have been in order until it was finalised. Then she could begin on the plans that she had only hinted at in the past few months.

With so many differing examples, how was a man to know what to do?

It was at times like this that he missed Gramp's advice. He did not always agree with it but it did allow him to see a situation clearly. He just needed to sort out his priorities, which was easier said than done while his emotions were in such a mess.

With no immediate solution to mind, he did the next best thing and went up to the study to write to his mother. There had been a letter for him on arrival today that he had not yet had time to read. Perhaps news of home and all that was familiar would help put things into perspective.

Lois had gone up to her private parlour. She sat down in front of George's portrait as she had done many times since his death. Her talks with him were not always in words. She just let her thoughts flow and waited for the comforting illusions of not being alone. Today those thoughts were like a raging torrent, sweeping her along as helpless as a rudderless boat. It was frightening, like being a small, confused child again just as she had been after her father died.

Lois liked a quiet life, free from unexpected hazards. George had given her that. Every problem had a solution if you thought back to the root cause.

That was easy.

Laington.

When she thought about Laington it was immediately overlaid with an image of George. The two were indivisible. They were her foundation, her way of life. She had never considered how she felt about them individually.

Noah's arrival had changed everything. It had changed her. He had made her look at things from a different perspective. Instead of acceptance she now had questions.

Did she love Laington for itself or because it epitomised George? And was her love for George based on gratitude? That thought felt so disloyal Lois made silent apology.

It had maybe started that way but George was basically lovable for himself.

So is Noah, her conscience prompted. Since his arrival she had been shaken out of her normal composure on numerous occasions. She did not know why she loved him. He could make her cross in a way no one else had ever done. People like Clive Grainger were mere irritants, easily dismissed. Noah and his thoughts and opinions were altogether different. She cared about the way he saw her and it was not always to her advantage. Did he intend to give her Laington because she loved it or was she just a convenient way of offloading something he did not want?

It occurred to her that was exactly what Ernest had done to George. George had no right to Laington or the barony. He had spent his life conserving it for Ernest and his descendants out of duty and affection.

She recalled Noah saying something he had learned from Ernest. It was to the effect that you only needed what you cared for. Nothing else mattered.

With blinding insight, Lois knew that was how she had always been treated. Her parents had not cared enough about her to put her needs above their own. Lady Charlotte had used her as unpaid help and a convenient, undemanding wife for her beloved son. Even George had ultimately used her as a way of ensuring the wellbeing of the estate.

Lois had never felt so insignificant and it was a relief to hear Sarah moving around in the dressing room, laying out her change of clothes for dinner.

With an enormous effort, Lois turned her back on the portrait. What was done was done. She was doomed to follow in George's footsteps, caring for an estate that was not hers out of duty and affection for the man who had loved and cared for her.

How different it would have been if Noah wanted Laington. She would have gladly helped him to assume control and then, finally, been free to consider her own needs. It was a bitter truth that she needed Noah, although he did not want or need her.

What she needed at this moment was to get a grip on her feelings and present a normal image at dinner. Having Mr Harris present would help. The man would be a buffer between herself and Noah. Whatever was finally decided, she did not want Noah to go with a bad opinion of her.

She did not want him to go at all.

Chapter 22

Lois found it difficult to engage Mr Harris's full attention. He was too fascinated by his surroundings. One of his first comments on arrival had been on the grandeur.

In the drawing room, his eyes roved the cabinets and paintings, and he commented on their provenance and estimated worth.

As soon as they entered the dining room, he went straight to the portrait of Charles II. After a close examination, he turned to Noah. 'One would never guess it was a copy if it were not signed and dated. I have seen the original Lely and cannot see any difference. But it does make a considerable difference to the value.'

'Thank you for telling me,' Noah said through gritted teeth. Lois could see he was annoyed but it did not seem to register with Mr Harris. The man acted more like an auctioneer than a lawyer. Did he think he was helping Noah to change his mind about leaving?

At the dining table, Lois half expected him to turn over the chinaware to inspect the maker's name or peer at the hallmark on the cutlery. His attitude irritated Lois but it made her think objectively and try to see the items through the eyes of a stranger.

She had grown up surrounded by beautiful and valuable objects and rarely considered them as individual items. But she did not take them for granted. She knew they were valuable although they were seldom spoken of in a monetary sense. They were treated with care and valued for their beauty. She had always known unconsciously that it was the artist's skill that made the difference between pottery and fine china. They were pleasant things to use and she was aware that other people did not eat from Spode plates or drink from crystal glasses. But did they make the food taste better? She did not think so. She had eaten pasties straight from a farmhouse oven with more relish than the chicken in aspic on her plate. Berries picked from a hedgerow were sweeter than the wine in her glass.

Bill had been stunned on arrival, but after his initial exploration, he preferred to be elsewhere. Mr Harris's avid interest was making Lois feel slightly uncomfortable. She tried to recall something Bill had said earlier. She could not remember exactly but, in essence, Bill saw no value in the things because he did not want them. Mr Harris was envious.

Lois had been so lost in her thoughts she did not realise she had stopped eating until Noah asked if she was unwell.

Lois shook her head and apologised. 'I was making lists in my head,' she prevaricated. 'There is a lot to do before Hattie's wedding.' She caught Noah's grin. He knew she was lying.

'There really is,' she said, defending herself, and she turned to Mr Harris. 'I hope you have been able to legalise her wishes.'

Mr Harris pursed his lips. 'I would not normally discuss one client's affairs with another but Miss Brown said you were aware of what she intended.'

'Yes, and I have already told her that Laington Grace is hers for life. She cannot give it away.' Lois shot a quick, accusing glance at Noah.

'That is correct. As for the income…' The lawyer shook his head. 'Miss Brown is not my usual class of client and I felt a duty to offer some advice.' His tone and rigid posture indicted that it had not been well received.

'I think employing an extra teacher is a wonderful use for the money,' Lois commented.

That part was news to Noah. 'Bill, Mr Norton, is a fine example of the difference education can make. When he was denied formal education, he observed and has acquired a wisdom I find admirable.'

'I did not detect that,' Mr Harris said scornfully. 'I told Miss Brown that a regular income would help to improve her husband's standing. I do not know his background but he has some way to go before he could be considered a gentleman.'

And thank God for that, Noah thought. Aloud he said, 'That depends upon how you measure a gentleman.'

Mr Harris had enough sense to recognise that the criticism had been, very politely, turned back on him, and he changed the subject.

Lois forgot to be aloof and looked at Noah to mouth, 'Bravo!'

The meal limped to a close with banal comments on the weather and the efficiency of the railway system.

Lois could not bear another moment of Mr Harris's company and agreed to his request for the use of a desk to draft out Hattie's bequests. She planned to escape to her room after showing him the into the office, but Noah was blocking her way to the stairs when she returned to the hall.

'I am not going to talk to you until after I have consulted Mr Harris,' she said firmly.

Noah quirked an eyebrow. 'You prefer his company to mine? I am hurt.'

Lois was hard put not to laugh at his attempt at a solemn expression. 'No, you are not! Now, please stand aside. You may have the pleasure of Mr Harris's company when he has finished his work.'

Lois had to brush past Noah when he only took a small step back. The temptation to turn into his arms was so great, Lois actually groaned. Noah's start of surprise gave her the opportunity to run up the stairs and away from temptation.

Now Noah really was hurt. Being close to him seemed to have caused Lois real distress. After her approval of his giving Mr Harris a set down, he had thought her attitude was softening. He sighed and returned to the drawing room with only another tedious hour with the lawyer to look forward to. He wished he could avoid it but courtesy demanded that he at least stay to wish the man goodnight.

With nothing else to do, Noah let his mind drift back to the letter he had received from his mother. It puzzled him a little as she wrote as though she assumed he would be staying in England. He could not think what had given her that impression. He had sent several letters with details of what he had been doing and the reasons for his extended visit, but he could not recall ever saying it would be permanent. He had included sketches of Laington, Lois, Bill and a few other people who had made an impression on him. Perhaps they had revealed more than intended. Or, as in the case of Simon Laing's portrait, hinted at things that could not be said.

Given the length of time it took to exchange letters, he did not know when his feelings for Lois had begun to dominate his drawing. He would remove his latest pictures from the letter he had written today and stress that he would be returning as soon as possible after Bill and Hattie's wedding.

Noah's thoughts were interrupted when Bill poked his head around the door and surveyed the room. 'Good,' he said before entering and closing the door. 'I was not going to come in if he was here.'

There was no need to ask to whom he was referring. Bill sat down opposite Noah and gave vent to his feelings.

'He as good as said I need Hattie's money to drag me out of the gutter! I told him I could stand on my own two feet!'

'Calm down.' Had it been anyone else, Noah would have offered a strong drink, but Bill was het up enough already. 'I have already heard Harris's version.'

Bill took a deep breath. His hands unclenched, his shoulders relaxed and his face became a blank mask. Noah surmised this was the face he had shown the lawyer.

'Sorry,' Bill said a moment later. 'I haven't felt so...' He struggled to find the right words.

'Diminished,' Noah supplied.

'Yeah. I'm done with being treated as worthless.'

'Quite right too.'

Noah would have added more but the source of Bill's annoyance chose that moment to join them.

Mr Harris was carrying a large bundle of papers tied with pink tape, and he had a determined expression. He ignored Bill and said, 'Lord Laing, I need to speak to you privately.'

Bill got up. 'Looks like you are in for a lecture, Noah. Best of luck.' He grinned at Noah behind Harris's back and left the room.

'What is so urgent it cannot wait until morning?' Noah asked.

'I wondered if you are aware of the extent of the property you want to give to Mrs Laing?' He jiggled the papers. 'This is a copy of the inventory taken after the late baron's death. Have you been shown the original?'

Noah shook his head. Lois had taken every opportunity to point things out but had not landed the whole thing on him at once. His comment about acting like a schoolteacher had obviously taken root. 'I don't need to see it. The only thing I intend to take away is the portrait of my grandfather.'

Mr Harris tutted. 'Irresponsibility appears to an infection at Laington. The late baron's will was ill-advised to say nothing of Lady Laing leaving property to a maid.'

Noah had heard enough. 'You seem to have plenty to say. I was under the impression that a lawyer carried out his clients' wishes.'

'We have a duty to offer advice where it is needed,' Harris spluttered. 'Once a will or deed is finalised there is no going back.'

'So be it. I will draft my own wishes after I have spoken to Mrs Laing.' Noah stood up. 'Pound will supply refreshments or anything else you need. Goodnight.'

He left the lawyer standing open mouthed in the middle of the room.

Noah's annoyance evaporated before he reached the top of the stairs. Gramp had taught him that everyone was entitled to their own opinion. It was how that opinion was delivered that mattered. Reasoned arguments were one thing; forcing your views onto someone else was plain rudeness. No wonder Bill had been so irate. Harris's manner reminded Noah unpleasantly of his father. He had had to bear those lectures, but he was not prepared to take them from someone else.

Noah came down early next morning, determined to speak to Lois before Harris could give any more unwanted advice.

Lois had risen even earlier and was waiting for him. She had abandoned her new gowns and wore what Noah thought of as one of her schoolmarm dresses of severely styled dark grey. And she looked ready for battle.

'I need to speak to you,' she said before he reached the bottom of the stairs. She marched into her office expecting him to follow. Noah took his time and she was seated behind the desk by the time he closed the door. Noah stood before the desk with his hands behind his back and the meekest expression he could manage, hoping to hide his amusement.

'Oh, for goodness' sake! Sit down!' Lois waited for him to pull up a chair. 'It is about your giving me Laington.' Noah nodded and waited. 'You cannot do it.' Lois raised her hand to forestall any comment. 'You do not have the authority to make any drastic changes.' Lois sat back as though that was the end of the matter.

Noah was taken aback for a moment until he remembered the terms of George's will. 'That is easily settled. You hand everything over to me and I give it back.'

'No. I can't remember the exact words but George meant me to stay as trustee until you were ready to take care of your inheritance.'

'I thought you would be pleased. What about all those improvements you want to make?'

'I can still do them. I only delayed because I did not know your views. You have said enough about the benefits of education for me to go ahead and turn the north wing into a proper school. You have shown no interest in redecoration or garden improvements, so they can go ahead too. I will do my best to care for Laington as trustee but I will not accept a massive gift I am not entitled to.'

Noah could almost see SO THERE! written in capitals above her head. He did not know whether to laugh or tear his hair out by the roots. She had him over the proverbial barrel. Any attempt to challenge the status quo would result in the whole lot going to the Crown, who had more than enough already. He ought to feel angry but was filled instead with a strange sense of relief. He did not understand it and stood when Lois suggested they go into breakfast.

During their absence, Bill and Harris had arrived in the breakfast room. The shape of the table did not allow them much distance but each was studiously ignoring the other. Bill looked up to say good morning and Harris got to his feet.

'Please continue with your breakfast,' Lois said cheerfully. 'Hattie will be here soon and you will want to be ready to start.'

Hattie arrived a few minutes later. She bustled into the room with apologies for her early arrival. She looked at Harris. 'What you said yesterday made me think. When Lady Charlotte left me Laington Grace, she did not give me anything to maintain it. So I want my annuity to go towards its upkeep. The extra teacher can live there rent free so will not need more than a basic wage.'

Hattie looked very pleased with herself and waited for the lawyer to comment. Harris nodded and gave a wary look at Bill before he answered. 'That can be arranged. I will word it in such a way that it may be changed in the future if necessary.'

Having settled what he considered to be a minor matter, Harris turned to Noah. 'Are you ready to discuss your affairs, my lord?'

Bill stood up. 'We'll get out of your way.' He guided Hattie from the room and shut the door. It reopened again to admit a maid, who asked if they needed more tea or coffee.'

Mr Harris opened his mouth but Noah forestalled him. 'I suggest we go through to the office. The staff need to clear. Will you come too?' he asked Lois.

Once in the office, Noah did not allow Mr Harris a chance to speak. 'There is really nothing to discuss. Mrs Laing has declined to accept a transfer of ownership and wishes to carry on as trustee.'

Harris looked at Lois in amazement. 'You declined? I tried to point out to Lord Laing the magnitude of the estate but it did not sway him. You, I assume, are more aware of its value.' He tapped the inventory.

'That is the very reason I declined. I cannot accept it. Noah's circumstances may change in the future. It is best not to do anything that cannot be reversed.'

'In that case I will just formalise Miss Brown's wishes and return to London.' Noah and Lois left him to it but Lois was still not entirely happy. 'Did you go through the inventory?' she asked when they were back in the drawing room.

'There was no need. I only want Gramp's portrait.'

'You ought to take the Laington ring. It has been used as a seal for more than two hundred years.

Noah rubbed his fingers over the ring on his right hand. 'I have worn this for less than two years but it means the world to me. I will wear it until the day I die.'

Lois had noticed many times the way he touched the ring when he was thinking or in moments of stress. She wished she had such a talisman. That was useless thinking and she needed a distraction. Fortunately, there was a lot to do before Hattie's wedding tomorrow. She used that as an excuse to leave the room.

Preparing for Hattie's wedding was a bitter-sweet experience for Lois. She wished her friend every happiness, but it underlined her own lonely future. She collected the basket of flowers the gardener had picked and drove her pony cart into town.

There were quite a few women already in the church. They had brought greenery and odd bits of ribbon to decorate the ends of the pews. Lois was touched. The ordinary folk did not have a lot to share but they looked after their own. Hattie was a staunch member of the Charity Society, willing to enter the poorer homes scorned by the more refined ladies.

It was accepted that Lois would arrange the flowers on the altar and they worked together, chatting about Hattie and how she would be missed. They spoke casually about her supposed liaison with George and Lois heard one woman say, 'Some people won't be able to look down their noses at her once she is married.' Another added, 'She deserves a chance of happiness. I could not have put up with you-know-who for so many years.' There was a general tittering and Lois realised they were referring to Lady Charlotte when someone said, 'His Lordship was a happier man when she was gone.'

Lois pretended not to hear. It was heartwarming that they felt able to gossip in her presence, but she could not actually join in. It was an example of her ambiguous status. She had known them all for years when she was just the orphan taken into the noble household. Her marriage to Simon had raised her slightly but, with Noah's advent, she was again reduced to a mere tenant. But everyone still treated her with friendly respect. It occurred to Lois that their show of respect for the baroness in her lifetime had not been genuine.

As Lois started to gather up the cuttings, one of the women said cheerfully, 'I'll see to that, Mrs Laing.' She inspected Lois's arrangement. 'Oh, that's nice.' The offer of help and simple compliment almost brought Lois to tears.

She allowed the tears to fall as she drove back to the manor. Not many, just a release of the feelings she had been hiding. She had never asked for pity and would not start now. With that resolve, she was able to face the rest of her arrangements with a smile.

The smile became more of an effort when Mr Harris sought her out.

'Mrs Laing, I have completed my business. It has been a pleasure to meet you. I am always at your service. You may call on me for advice at any time.'

Lois shook his hand and managed not to actually accept his offer. He was nothing like his father and she did not like him. She would tell Noah she intended transferring the estate business to a local lawyer. It would be more convenient and she had dealt with Mr Burrows regarding her own assets.

Mr Harris took a lingering glance around before Pound politely shepherded him out of the door, which he shut before the carriage had pulled away. He gave Lois a satisfied nod and she watched him walk away. She had to smile. Pound was too controlled to comment but he was obviously glad to see the back of the lawyer.

It was another lesson in not underestimating the intelligence of those considered inferior. Respect had to be earned. Mr Harris had not actually been rude to the staff, but he never showed any appreciation and had taken Lois's remark to ask for anything he required to heart.

'Has he gone?'

Lois looked up to where Noah was leaning over the gallery rail. 'You did not come down to see him on his way,' she accused.

Noah started to walk towards the stairs. 'I said all that was necessary when I witnessed Hattie's will. I was on my way down to give you this.' Noah held up the case of George's letters.

'There is no need. Leave them in the study and I will put them away after you have… I will put them away later.' Lois could not bring herself to mention his leaving. Noah turned back and Lois fled to the kitchen.

'I have come to look at the cake,' she said as she entered the kitchen.

Betty to the pantry and threw open the larder door with a flourish. 'There,' she said smugly. 'I've used a month's sugar but don't you think it was worth it?'

The bride cake was a work of art, frosted with sugar swirls and garlands. 'I only did one tier. Hattie's not likely to have children.' Betty explained the old tradition of keeping one tier of the wedding cake for the Christening of the first child. Lois fleetingly wondered what had happened to the saved tier of her bride cake. She hoped whoever had eaten it had enjoyed it more than the morsel she had forced down.

'It is beautiful,' she told the cook. 'Bill will enjoy it. He has a very sweet tooth.'

Lois turned her attention to the two marzipan figures on top of the cake. 'Oh, they are perfect. I am glad you have made them so lifelike. I am sure Hattie will want to keep them.'

'If she can stop Bill from eating them!' The kitchen maids joined in Betty's laughter. Unlike the recently departed lawyer, Bill was well liked by the staff.

Betty shooed the maids back to their work. 'We still have the pies to do. I don't want to be in the kitchen while my sister is getting married.'

It was Lois's signal to leave.

She was not needed for the next task on her list. Mrs Collins met her in the hall. 'I have just checked the Mozart room is ready for the new Mr and Mrs Norton. They did not have very long for a honeymoon.'

'I think being at Bill and Hattie's wedding was more important.'

'And they will have a long journey before they start their new lives in Australia.'

It was another reminder of things Lois was trying hard not to think about. She needed to do something completely unrelated to weddings and departures. Before she could make a decision, Noah emerged from the office holding a large envelope.

'The sailing details have arrived.'

Lois had to swallow the lump in her throat before she could speak. 'When is it to be?'

'On the twenty-third of April. Less than a week. We will need to get to Southampton the day before.' Noah did not sound very excited about it.

'St George's Day.' Lois gave a rueful laugh. 'That seems appropriate.'

Noah looked at her sharply. It was not like Lois to be sarcastic. He felt guilty but could not think exactly why. He had told her from the start that he would be leaving. It was an awkward moment. He wanted to say he was sorry but was not sure exactly why. He hefted the envelope and said, 'I will take this upstairs.'

Lois watched him mount the stairs. Once again she was at a loose end with too much time to think. Every task had connections to his leaving so she might as well do something towards that end. With a determined step, Lois called for a footman to accompany her upstairs.

Noah was in the library, selecting a few books to read on the voyage. He would check with Lois that they were not particular favourites but, after all, she had made it plain that he was still the owner and free to take anything he wished.

His browsing was disturbed by the sound of movement and voices in the gallery. He frowned. It was unusual for any of the staff to be in this part of the house during the afternoon.

Curiosity made him go to the door to investigate.

Lois, a footman and a maid were a bit further along the galley, talking earnestly.

Lois turned as he walked towards them. They were clustered in front of Gramp's portrait.

'I was about to have your picture packed up but it seems to be stuck fast,' Lois explained.

The footman took up the story. 'I will have to damage either the frame or the wall.'

Noah took a close look. It appeared that, sometime in the past, the wall had been repainted without removing the picture first. He took the footman's screwdriver and poked at the paint. Whatever its composition, it was set rock hard.

'When was the wall repainted?'

'I have no idea,' Lois replied. 'I don't remember it being done since I arrived and George would never have condoned such shoddy workmanship. Which would you prefer, damage to the wall or the frame?'

Before replying, Noah went to examine several of the other portraits. Some of the larger pictures were only stuck at the bottom where the paint had accumulated. Where it was possible, he peered behind the frames. In every case the painted area only extended for a few inches behind the picture. It made his decision easier. 'They all present the same problem. I suggest a complete inspection by a competent builder. He may have a solvent. If not, I am afraid the wall will have to suffer.' He looked around. 'A complete redecoration would not come amiss and the pictures could be cleaned at the same time. I doubt they have been touched since they were created.'

Lois smiled brightly. 'I have often thought the older ones looked dingy.' She spoke to the servants. 'We will leave things for now. I will get Hemmings to contact a reliable builder as soon as possible.'

Having dealt with the problem as far as possible, Lois sent the servants away. 'I am afraid it cannot be tomorrow. I am not sure how many people will return after the wedding service but we cannot have workmen here at the same time. Whatever happens, your picture will be safely packed up before you leave.'

She cannot wait to get rid of me, Noah thought sadly. On second thoughts, perhaps having a project to concentrate on would help Lois to get back to normal.

'While you are up here,' Noah said when Lois made to follow the servants, 'I have been choosing some reading material for the journey. Will you cast your eyes over my selection?' He expected her to remind him that he could take anything he wanted, but she just nodded and entered the library.

Instead of looking at the small pile of books on the table, Lois scanned the shelves searching for gaps. Satisfied that he had not taken any of the books George had bought specially for her, she said, 'That does not look very many. And perhaps Bill might like some for himself. Books are the only things in the house he has shown any interest in.'

'Good idea. I can hardly believe how his reading has improved. When I first met him he had to sound out each word.'

Lois nodded. 'I wonder what he could have achieved if things had been different.' She fell silent, mentally comparing the bumbling, insecure man who had arrived with the happy, confident Bill of today. Life could be so unfair. She pushed aside the uncomfortable thought and said brightly, 'Do you know what time Fred and Ruby expect to arrive?'

'I told Fred we could arrange to meet them at the Halt, but he preferred to make his own arrangements.' Noah spoke absently as he was still studying the bookshelves. He did not hear Lois quietly leave the room. When he turned, she was gone but he caught the sound of soft footsteps and went to the door.

Lois was standing in front of George's portrait. As he watched, she reached out and touched the frame, which moved under her hand. 'I thought so!' Lois was talking to the picture and sounded very pleased. She turned away and stopped in surprise when she saw Noah in the doorway. 'George's picture is not stuck so the wall must have been painted before he inherited.'

'That pleases you?'

'I suppose it does. George was meticulous and inspected any ongoing work.' She shrugged her shoulders. 'He never actually criticised his father but they had completely different attitudes towards the estate. Arthur Laing, as far as I can tell, was a very social person and only used Laington for entertaining. He spent most of his time in London but there was a period' – Lois chuckled – 'George called it the regency, between the eleventh baron becoming frail and George being old enough to take charge. I can only suppose the redecoration was done then.'

'Have you ever been to London?' Noah asked curiously.

'Of course.' Lois laughed. 'I have not been a prisoner! It was fun for a while but I found endless parties rather a waste of time. No one seemed to have any objective beyond being the centre of attention. I'm sorry. That sounds priggish.'

'Not at all. I entirely agree with you.' Noah enjoyed these moments when Lois dropped her guard. He would have been happy to continue the conversation but sounds from the hall heralded the arrival of the newlyweds.

'We picked Bill up,' Fred announced when they joined the newlyweds in the hall. 'He was tramping back from town.'

'I have been to buy Hattie a ring!' The big man grinned and patted his pocket. 'I can't wait for tomorrow.'

'I can recommend marriage.' Fred pulled Ruby closer to his side. Ruby's sometimes plain face almost glowed as she gazed at her new husband.

Lois felt a pang of envy. Two days after her own marriage she had been crying and racked with guilt.

Noah watched the sudden sadness in Lois's expression. Was she thinking of her own brief marriage? It would be even worse for her tomorrow. He wished… There was no point in pursuing that thought, and Noah put himself to the task of being a good host.

Dinner that evening was a lively meal. Most of the conversation centred on the fast-approaching journey. Fred insisted on paying for his own and Ruby's passage. Before Bill could offer to do the same, Noah said, 'Bill will be working his passage again. If it is anything like the way here, he will be taking care of me!' Everyone laughed and Noah looked at his friend. 'I would not have survived without you and I am not setting foot on a boat without you.' He forestalled Bill's protest by adding lightly, 'And they don't want to hear all the gory details.'

'I was surprised that Bill is so keen to go back to Australia,' Ruby remarked.

'It is a good place if you are free and willing to work,' Bill assured her.

Lois changed the subject. 'We thought you might like to choose some books to occupy you on the journey.'

Bill was delighted and wanted to go up straight away. 'You should see the library, Fred. I won't know where to start.'

'You still have plenty of time. Concentrate on tomorrow.'

Bill almost blushed. 'I've not thought about much else,' he admitted. 'Hattie has told me not to visit this evening. She said she had things to do.' His faced creased in a frown of puzzlement. 'I thought it was all arranged.'

Ruby touched his arm. 'She will probably be just as excited as you. I don't know her very well yet but she told me about her secret marriage to the baron. Tomorrow will be so different.'

'Very different,' Lois agreed. 'Hattie thinks it will be quiet but the townspeople will turn out to wish her well.' She told them of the morning activities, stressing how much Hattie was going to be missed. Before anyone could say she would also miss Hattie, Lois told them of the marzipan figures on the wedding cake and warned Bill that he was not to eat them.

Chapter 23

Bill woke at his usual time next day. Years of enforced early rising were too ingrained for him to sleep late now he had a chance. He got up and was just pulling on his trousers when Pound and the two footmen arrived with cans of hot water.

On his first morning at Laington, Bill had been surprised and slightly horrified that the staff thought he expected to be waited upon. Since then he had formed a habit of taking down his own slops and washing in the room attached to laundry. His unassuming manner and willingness to help had endeared him to the staff and, today, they had taken matters into their own hands.

'Good morning, Mr Norton. We have come to get you ready for your wedding,' Pound told him, suppressing a grin.

'I am going to trim your hair and give you a proper shave,' Bush, the elder footman, added, examining Bill's razor and stropping it on the leather. 'Please sit down.'

The younger footman, who had left the room, returned with Bill's best suit. 'I have steamed and pressed it. And polished your boots' He laid the suit across the end of the bed and went to the chest of drawers. 'I got the laundry maids to starch your shirt. We want you looking as fine as fivepence.'

Bill meekly submitted to being treated like a lord. He was overwhelmed that anyone, apart from Hattie, would care how he looked. An hour later the servants stood back as Bill surveyed himself in the mirror. 'I look like a proper gent,' he said quietly and turned to thank them.

Pound gave him a fatherly smile. 'It has been our pleasure, sir. We all wish you every happiness.'

Bill was still trying to thank them when they filed out of the door. He turned back to the mirror. He could not quite put his finger on why he looked so different, not that he had ever spent much time looking at himself. He rubbed a hand over his smooth cheeks. Bush had wrapped a hot towel around his face before applying the lather and some kind of stinging lotion after the shave. Bill had tried to be presentable but his usual quick scrape did not compare.

What Bill did not see was the change in his posture. The suit that had always felt too good for him now sat comfortably and the starched collar of the shirt lifted his chin a fraction. He did not have the words to describe how he felt but being treated with so much affection and respect had made him more of a man.

Lois, Fred and Ruby were already seated at the breakfast table when Noah joined them. 'Has Bill finished already?' he asked after he had said good morning.

Lois pointed to the clean place setting. 'He has not come down yet.'

Noah frowned. Bill was usually the first to arrive and had often finished and set off for work by this time.

'Shall I go up and see what's keeping him?' Fred suggested. 'Perhaps he has got cold feet and plans to run away.'

He went to the door and was almost bowled over when it opened with a flourish. Pound stood to one side to allow Bill to enter.

They all stared.

'I've been seen to,' Bill explained sheepishly.

'You have indeed,' Noah told him.

Fred returned things to normal by punching his brother on the arm. 'Make sure you don't get messed up before the wedding.' He laughingly tucked a napkin under Bill's chin. 'We don't want you spilling food down your clean shirt.'

Bill protested. 'I don't slop my food!' But he did not remove the napkin until he had finished eating.

'What are we supposed to do now?' Bill asked when they left the room. 'It is too early to go to the church.'

'Ruby and I are going to get changed then we are taking Betty down to Laington Grace. And the staff need to get ready too.'

'Hattie said she did not want any fuss but we are family now,' Ruby added. 'Brides get fussed whether they like it or not!'

It was a beautiful day. An example of the English spring poets wrote about. The sun shone from a blue sky dotted with fluffy white clouds. A gentle breeze carried the scent of warm earth and new growth. The mood was enhanced by the cheerful voices of the house servants as they climbed into the drey and old travelling coach which Farmer had cleaned up for the occasion.

The modern carriage had returned from taking Lois, Ruby and Betty to see Hattie and stood at the door ready to take Fred and Bill to the church. It was not highly decorated but it shone with polish and the horses had white plumes on their heads.

Noah watched them go with relief. Keeping Bill occupied for the last couple of hours had been tiring. The empty house felt different when he went inside. For the first time he was the sole occupant. It ought to have been uncomfortable but, strangely, Noah felt more at home now than ever before.

With nothing else to do for a while, Noah wandered from room to room. He had not previously been much interested in the house contents. The land he could understand but possessions had never figured largely in his life. He had not missed them while he was travelling with Gramp; there had always been so much else to see and learn. He had despised Mr Harris's mercenary attitude but now it made him see things in a different light.

Had Gramp's scorn for possessions been a reaction to having been banished from all this? He had spent part of his youth here, a member of the family and in line for the title.

Noah came to a halt in front of the family portrait Lois had mentioned. It was signed 'A Donati' and dated 1786. Underneath was a faded card with the information – Arthur Laing, his wife Greta, sons Ernest and George, his sister Ashley.

Noah smiled and wondered how many people were aware of the significant arrangement. Arthur stood behind the chair of a stout woman with a placid face and blonde hair neatly arranged in coils over her ears. She had her arm around a young boy who was obviously Ernest. The other woman, by contrast, was slender and had the typical Laing features. Her dress was elaborate and her hair a mass of curls. On her lap was a curly-haired infant. Reflected in the mirror behind them was the image of the chubby, laughing artist at his easel.

It was a true family portrait, mothers and children painted by the infants' father. Ashley and Antonio had allowed their son to be adopted but given him a picture to treasure. Noah wondered if George had ever been told.

There was no time for further speculation as a shout from the hall warned him that it was time for him go.

Hattie was ready and waiting. Noah got down to help her into the carriage thinking she and Bill would make a striking pair. Hattie's lavender-coloured dress was quite plain compared to her usual taste for frills and flounces. The only decoration was piping of a darker shade and the way the material was drawn up into a bustle. A small hat with an upturned brim in matching material gave the impression of a tiara, without the sparkle. Overall, she looked more regal than bridelike although there was a certain tension in the way she moved.

Noah bowed. 'My lady, your carriage awaits.'

'I hope Bill is waiting as well. I lay awake last night thinking he would get cold feet.'

'We almost had to tie him down to stop him going to church directly after breakfast!'

The carriage had only gone a few yards when Hattie said, 'Stop! Stop the carriage!'

'Have you just had second thoughts?' Noah asked in surprise.

'No, of course not! I need to talk to you.' Hattie seemed uncertain of how to start. Taking a deep breath, she faced Noah and said, 'There is something you ought to know. I don't suppose it will make any difference but I don't want to carry George's secrets into my new marriage.'

Noah nodded, wondering what could be so important Hattie was willing to be late for her own wedding. amazement. 'George was adopted,' Hattie muttered. 'He found the certificate among his dead father's possessions.' Hattie paused for breath and Noah touched her hand. 'I know. Ernest was nearly eight years of age when George was born. Old enough to know that his mother had not been pregnant at that time.'

'That is not all,' Hattie insisted. 'It played on his mind so much that when Lois was to marry Simon, George gave me the adoption certificate. If he died before Ernest or his heirs returned.

I was to use it to prove that…' Hattie stopped. 'I am not putting this very well. George was so riddled guilt he was prepared to disinherit his own son!'

'As you say, it does not change anything and no longer matters. It does explain why George started searching for Ernest as soon as he inherited. Does Lois know?'

'I don't think so.'

Parker opened the hatch in the roof. 'Do you want me to drive on? We are going to be very late.'

'The bride is allowed to be late,' Hattie told him. 'But it is not fair to keep Bill waiting too long.' Sathe smiled at Noah. 'I am glad to have got that off my chest. What you do with the knowledge is none of my business.' Having was almost gay as they continued the short journey.

The area in front of the church was deserted and Hattie's face fell as she glanced around. Noah could almost feel her disappointment. There were usually curious onlookers at any wedding and Lois had expected a crowd of friends to be there to wish Hattie well.

Noah offered Hattie his arm and they climbed the church steps. Organ music started before they were actually through the door overlaying the sound of movement. Noah paused to allow Hattie to take in the scene. He felt her tremble and looked down in time to see her blink away a tear.

The large church was not packed but a good crowd filled the pews closest to the aisle.

As they continued their progress, Bill turned to watch them. He took a step forward and there was a spontaneous outbreak of applause.

After doing his duty of giving the bride away, Noah slipped into a seat just behind Lois and Betty. A quick glance around told him Lois had been right. Hattie might only have one sister but she had lots of friends.

At the end of the service, Noah and Fred accompanied the couple into the vestry to sign the register. When they emerged, the majority of the congregation had gone outside, leaving just a few close friends to follow Bill and Hattie back down the aisle.

'I think that went well,' Noah remarked as he offered Lois his arm.

'Yes. As proxy father of the bride will you invite anyone who wishes to come to the manor for refreshments?'

Behind her, Betty muttered, 'We will have to ration the sandwiches.'

People crowded around the newlyweds, offering congratulations. Very few of them were able to accept Noah's invitation as they had to return to work. It spoke of real friendship that they had taken the time to attend.

Hattie had not carried flowers so there was no tossing of the bouquet, but Lois slipped away and collected a small bunch of spring flowers from the stone bench in the porch. Noah watched her take it to George's large tomb and stand for a moment before laying the flowers. She appeared to be speaking, although he was too far away to hear. Noah had seen her do the same thing after Sunday service and noted that the tribute was always for George, not her husband.

Ruby came to stand beside him. 'These weddings must be so hard for Lois, reminding her of her own wedding. I wonder why her husband died so young.'

Noah had often wondered the same thing. John Partridge had spoken of an accident but implied it had not been fatal. He had said Simon had changed but Noah had no idea in what way. There was a conspiracy of silence around the young heir and it did not feel like regret.

Lois joined them. 'We need to get back to the manor ahead of the others,' she said briskly, as though they had been keeping her waiting. 'Our carriage is here.'

Noah was not accustomed to arranging events and had not given any thought as to how they were to return to the manor. Bill and Hattie were being waved off in the now highly decorated Laington carriage, but a modest vehicle came to a halt beside them. The driver tipped his hat and the ladies were helped to board.

'This is the same carriage that brought us from the station,' Fred remarked and closed the door.

'I have arranged for it to be available if you want to show Ruby around the area.'

'I would like to explore the church,' Ruby said enthusiastically. 'I like old buildings and I do not suppose there is anything like it in Australia.' Noah agreed. The continent was still largely unpopulated but efforts were being made to erect fine buildings in the most prominent towns.

They took the short route back to the manor and were standing on the front steps when Bill and Hattie arrived, closely followed by those who had come to celebrate. It was a rare treat for the working people to be entertained inside the manor and they were rather subdued. It was so unlike Fred and Ruby's boisterous reception. Ruby spoke of the difference and asked Lois, 'Were they a bit livelier at your wedding?'

Lois shook her head. 'They were not invited. The family was in mourning for the late baroness.'

Hattie put her arm around Lois's shoulders and almost glared at Ruby. 'It was more like a wake and Lois does not need reminding.'

Lois brushed aside Ruby's apology. 'It was a long time ago. We don't want any dismal thoughts today.' She took Ruby's hand. 'Come and help me pass around the refreshments.'

Noah and the brothers were standing close by and Bill asked Hattie, 'Was it really so bad? I don't like to think of Lois being unhappy.'

'There has not been much happiness in her life and it is going to get even worse.' Hattie gave Noah a curt nod and hurried after Lois.

The three men exchanged uncomfortable glances. Something was very wrong and they had no idea how to help.

The guests did not stay long. Lois did her best to put the guests at ease and was unusually gay as she spoke of the wonderful adventures Hattie would have in her new home. It seemed to work but once the cake had been admired and cut, toasts drunk and Hattie and Fred had slipped away to some private rendezvous, they collected small portions of cake to take to those unable to be present and went away.

Lois breathed a sigh of relief when they were all gone. All she wanted to do was go to bed and cry. But there was still dinner to get through and the staff had made every effort to turn it into a gala occasion. As a result, Lois drank a little more wine than usual.

As soon as the meal was over, Hattie kissed Lois's cheek and thanked her for a lovely day. Very shyly Bill did the same before hurrying Hattie from the room. Lois knew she ought to see them off but felt a little dizzy and stayed where she was and left the goodbyes to Fred and Ruby. The couple were also eager to be alone and did not return, leaving Lois with Noah.

When Lois made the effort to stand, she swayed and Noah quickly took her arm and led her to the drawing room. He sat beside her on one of the deep couches and asked the silliest question ever. 'Are you alright?'

Lois's laugh turned into a sob and she willingly accepted the comfort of Noah's arms. He rocked her and, unable to find any words of comfort, simply offered his large handkerchief. He waited until the storm of weeping had passed, tormented by her grief but reluctant to let her out of his arms.

Lois finally lifted her head, screwing the soggy linen into a ball. Her eyes were puffy and her nose red but Noah thought she had never looked more beautiful.

Lois gave a little hiccup and tried to smile. 'Thank you. I needed that. I was so worried I might spoil Hattie's day.'

'I think Hattie understood. The last thing she said to me was to make you talk.'

'Yes, it won't matter now.' She sounded so despairing Noah wanted to cry too. He tightened his arms and Lois relaxed against his chest with a sigh. Without looking at his she said, 'You want to know about Simon.'

Noah did not reply directly. 'I want to know why you are so unhappy, apart from losing Hattie.'

'I lose everyone. My father shot himself rather than face penury. My mother died of shame. Everyone thinks I loved Simon but he was not real. I was too naïve to realise he was selfish and spoilt by his mother.' She looked up and said defiantly, 'I killed him.'

Noah sat up in shock, almost knocking Lois from her seat. She laughed bitterly. 'Now you see why I won't talk about him. I deserve to be miserable. I caused his accident and left the laudanum where he could reach it. That was why George died in pain, because he was scared of becoming addicted too.'

She tried to stand and tugged against Noah's hand when he pulled her back. 'You can go now, back to a new land that is not tainted by the past.'

'I don't believe you,' he said quietly. 'Those may be the facts but they are not the story. You have come this far. Get rid of the rest of the burden you have been carrying.'

Lois was too weary to resist. Noah did not ask questions as, bit by bit, Lois took him though her life.

Lois had assumed guilt for her father's suicide and mother's decline as a sign that she was not worth living for. George had made her feel special and she had been willing to do anything not to lose that love. 'When he was dying, George said he was sorry for allowing me to marry Simon. He was disappointed in his son and thought I would make him a better man.' Lois snorted. 'I did the opposite. I defied him, made him so cross he was thrown from his horse. When he tried to shoot Jupiter, he was knocked down again and his hip never mended. He could not bear being an invalid and ignored by his friends. He became addicted to the laudanum and kept begging for more. One day I left the bottle where he could reach it.'

Noah accepted the bare facts. The clues had been scattered in his path like a scent trail. The portrait of Simon Laing showed arrogance, petulance and a hint of cruelty. Parker had spoken of a misused horse who had been sold. He suspected John Partridge had only remained a friend to support Lois.

Lois had been silent for so long, Noah risked moving into a more comfortable position. She murmured and snuggled deeper into his arms, and he realised she had fallen asleep.

He was filled with a sense of peace and allowed his cheek to rest against her hair. The clock ticked, the candles burnt down, and he lost all sense of time until cramp forced him back to the present. As he flexed his fingers, his thumb rubbed against his ring.

He knew what he had to do – what he wanted to do – but there was not much time. He was due to leave in a matter of days and could not ask Lois to make a life-changing decision until she had recovered her strength.

The sound of the door opening made him turn his head to see Pound standing in the doorway. The butler advanced and Noah pursed his lips as a warning for him not to speak. Having reached the end of the couch, Pound could see Lois. His face softened and he whispered, 'I will fetch Sarah.'

Noah shook his head. 'No. Lead the way and I will carry her.' As gently as he could, Noah eased to the edge of the seat and rose with Lois in his arms. She stirred but did not wake until he lowered her down onto her bed.

Lois opened her eyes and smiled. It was such a lovely dream. If she moved her head a little she would be able to kiss him. She closed her eyes again and drifted away with the feel of his breath on her lips.

Noah straightened up reluctantly and backed away. Pound waited for him to leave the room and closed the door. 'Sarah will take care of her,' he whispered with a benign smile. 'Will you be needing anything more, my lord?'

Noah moved them further away from the door. 'Not tonight but I have a great deal of work for you tomorrow.' He said goodnight and went to his own room.

Chapter 24

Lois clung to the remnants of her dream until Sarah rolled her over to undo her dress. She started to struggle. 'Now, now, Miss Lois. You will be more comfortable in your nightgown.'

Sarah's voice swept away the last trace of sleep and Lois sat up. 'How did I…'

'Never mind that now. Lift your arms like a good girl. There we go.' Sarah kept up a soft stream of instructions as she undressed Lois and slipped the nightgown over her head, just as she had done so many years ago when Lois had arrived, a sad, frightened little girl. Once she had her mistress tucked under the covers, Sarah bent and kissed her cheek. Lois muttered a few words, already slipping back into sleep. Sarah waited until she was satisfied that Lois was not going to wake before she went in search of Pound.

Lois woke in the early hours, thirsty and in need of the commode. Those activities brought her to full consciousness and she began to gather her thoughts. She could not remember coming to bed, only that she'd had a beautiful dream. The details vanished as she tried to recall them, leaving a blank space between talking to Noah and now.

Lois felt her face redden as she remembered crying in his arms. What ever must he have thought of that outpouring of self-pity? How was she to face him in the morning? She groaned. It could not be avoided. Two days, three at the most to get through. Thank goodness Fred and Ruby were here. She would spend as much time as possible with them.

Lois found it hard to get back to sleep and made lists in her head. It usually worked to distract her mind when she was worried.

It did not work so well now. As a result, when she did fall asleep it was deeply, and she was later than usual getting up.

Sarah had peeped into her mistress's room at the usual hour and, seeing she was still fast asleep, diverted the maid with the hot water to Mr and Mrs Norton's room. Then she went and knocked on His Lordship's door.

Noah was surprised by the knock. He had made it plain to the footmen that he preferred to dress himself so they just left his washing water in the dressing room. He was even more surprised to see Lois's maid when he opened the door.

The elderly woman looked stern. 'Please excuse me, my lord, but I am about to be very impertinent.'

Noah tried not to laugh as he ushered her into the room. 'Go ahead.'

Sarah had rehearsed what she wanted to say but it was not easy. 'My lord, about last night. Lois said she had told you everything.'

Noah nodded and waited for the maid to continue.

'About Master Simon?' Noah nodded again. 'I doubt that,' Sarah said firmly. 'I tried to prepare her, to tell her what would happen, but I did not think even he would rape her.' Sarah clapped her hands over her mouth. She looked at Noah's shocked face and rushed on. 'She was torn and bleeding. She could not face getting on a horse to join the New Year hunt. She thinks it is her fault that he fell.'

Noah was shaking with anger and unable to speak. Thinking she had overstepped the mark, Sarah backed away. 'I am sorry for speaking out of turn. I just don't want her to be hurt anymore.' Sarah's tears ran unchecked down her cheeks, but her emotions had also been hidden for too many years.

Noah led her to a chair. 'I am not surprised she wanted to kill him.'

'No, no it was not like that,' Sarah insisted. 'Master Simon had always had his own way. The only person he heeded was his mother, who indulged him. He did not want to marry Lois, or anyone else. It was her wish. He was too much of a coward to defy her. So my poor girl went like a lamb to the slaughter.' Sarah gulped for breath. 'He was angry even before the vows were said. Later, when he could not move, he blamed Lois, said awful things and tried to hit her. One day she ran from the room and forgot to take the laudanum bottle. Somehow, he got out of bed. They found him on the floor with the empty bottle still in his hand. I don't suppose he meant to kill himself and the doctor hushed it up.'

Sarah stood up. 'That is all I have to say. You can dismiss me but I will come back the minute you are gone. I just did not want you to go away thinking Lois was a murderess.'

Noah took her hands. 'Thank you for telling me. I did not believe it happened the way Lois described.' He smiled reassuringly and helped Sarah to her feet. 'I am glad there are people who love and care for her.'

After the maid had gone, Noah sat down on the chair and put his head in his hands. He was grateful to the maid, but it made his task even harder. But he would find a way.

First of all, he needed to dress and speak to Pound.

Lois did not need to implement her lists. One of the younger maids brought her morning tea with the message that Sarah was feeling unwell. Nothing serious and she did not want Mrs Laing to worry.

On her way to breakfast, Lois was waylaid by the butler with the news that, 'The master has gone for an early ride.' Lois was not really surprised. He would not want to be in her company after last night.

Fred and Ruby had finished their breakfast but stayed to keep Lois company. Not that she had much of an appetite. 'Can you spare the time to show me around the house?' Ruby asked. 'How do you manage to run a place this size?'

'I don't actually do very much. As I told your mother, a good housekeeper and servants do the work. I just do the nice bits.'

Ruby kept up a light-hearted chatter as they went from room to room. She was more interested in the building than the contents, repeating that she liked old buildings and was quite knowledgeable. 'I liked our cottage in Whitby more than the Bristol house.'

'Modern houses have some advantages,' Lois insisted. 'I am thinking of having water piped to the upper floors and flushing lavatories. I am glad I never had to empty the pots!'

Lois took her guest to the office to look at catalogues of the latest plumbing. She had never met another woman who was interested in such things. These innovations were out of reach for her working-class friends, and others, in better circumstances, preferred to talk about fashion.

Noah did not return until nearly lunchtime. He seemed much as usual and he did not try to single Lois out. It ought to have reassured her but Lois wanted to know what he had made of her outburst, even if it was to her detriment. The pending conversation could not be put off forever. Fred and Ruby planned to explore the church and some of the other old buildings in Stapleton that afternoon and would be dining with Bill and Hattie at Laington Grace. She would be alone with Noah for dinner and resolved to be more sparing with the wine. It must have been the reason she had lost control yesterday. And there was still the afternoon to get through.

When they left, Lois retreated to her small office. There was always something that needed attention. Now her attention was illusive and her mind kept wandering back to the previous evening. Her memories of the early part of the dinner were quite clear. They had discussed the wedding and Hattie's surprise that so many people had attended. That had led to the reception. They recalled how the cake had been admired. Food was always an easy topic for Bill, and Hattie had told him to make the most of it as she was not a good cook. Ruby naturally wanted to know more about Molly, Hattie's housekeeper, who had been offered a post with Mrs Drayton. Hattie then invited Fred and Ruby to dine with her next day so they could meet Molly.

After the others left, Lois's recollections were blurred. She knew she had gone to the drawing room with Noah but could not remember what had caused her to start crying. It had shattered all of her defences, and years of guilt and worry had spilled out in a pathetic stream of self-pity. After that she only had the very vaguest impression of being held in Noah's arms, but that could have been part of her dream.

When she went up to change for dinner, Lois was aware of an odd atmosphere in the house. Everyone was smiling and she put it down to relief that yesterday's hectic activity was over. Sarah had recovered from her indisposition and Pound was more relaxed than she had ever known him. Dinner had been laid in the small dining room and whether from intent or habit, there was a jug of lemonade on the table. Pound poured her a glass without asking and Lois could not put a name to his smile. Fatherly did not occur to her, but it struck a long-forgotten chord from the happy days of her early childhood.

When the servants had left the room, and before picking up her soupspoon, Lois started to apologise for her behaviour the previous evening. Noah said there was no need and advised Lois to start her soup before it got cold.

'It is more convenient for the staff to serve us in here and less intimidating than being watched by a long-dead king,' Noah remarked. 'On my first exploration I was surprised to find what I thought was a kitchen next to the dining room. It is very useful to have somewhere to keep the food warm when the dining room is so far from the kitchen.'

Lois recognised, with relief, that this was an attempt to keep the conversation away from personal matters and told him of Ruby's interest in the subject of indoor plumbing. From then on it was easy to talk about trivial things.

Lois's tension returned after the meal was over and Noah suggested they retire to the drawing room. She went to her favourite seat on one of the sofas by the window and feigned interest in the way the soft evening twilight cast a magical glow on the garden.

Noah came to stand in front of her and looked at her for several seconds before speaking.

'Lois, we must talk about last night. No, don't apologise again. You have been burdened for too long. The upheaval of recent days and a glass or two of wine burst the dam.' Noah moved closer and crouched down so their eyes were on a level. He took hold of her hands and spoke quietly. 'You did not kill your husband. Odd things I have heard and my own observations add up to the fact that he was not a good man. For that matter, George was not quite the person you thought him.'

'How can you say that!' Lois protested, trying to free her hands. 'You never met him. He was kind and hardworking. He saw Laington as a trust that had to be preserved. Simon was a disappointment and George pinned all his hopes on you.'

'And I have failed?' Noah made it sound like a question. He stood up but still faced her. 'After I received his letter, I showed it to Gramp. He had never spoken much of his life in England but it appeared he had been hiding his feelings for years, and like you, needed to let them out. He felt guilty for leaving George to carry all the responsibility, but his love for my grandmother was more important than anything else.' Noah rubbed his ring. 'There is an inscription in here that sums everything up.' He slipped the ring from his hand and gave it to Lois. She held it closer to the window. On the inner surface of the ring was inscribed, *Love is all*.

Lois handed the ring back but could think of nothing to say. Noah was leading somewhere and she braced herself to hear the real reason he needed to return to Australia.

'Love is all,' Noah repeated. 'Do you believe that?'

Lois could only nod and Noah came back to kneel before her. 'Lois, I love you. Now I know why you are so scared of being touched, I must speak. I promise I will never hurt you. Can you learn to trust me? To learn to love me enough to marry me?'

Tears filled Lois's eyes. 'I don't need to learn. I have loved you for longer than I realised. I avoided you because I wanted you to kiss me again.'

Noah leaned forward and gratified her wish. It cost him an effort to keep it slow and tender. He had to woo Lois. Her terrible treatment had made her afraid of intimacy, but she did not try to get away. God willing, he would have time to teach her how wonderful love could be. Noah moved to look at her face and waited for an answer.

'Yes,' she said quietly.

'Even if it means leaving Laington?'

Lois thought for a moment before repeating, 'Yes.'

Noah swept her into his arms until they were almost lying the length of the sofa and kissed her with pent-up passion. Lois's response started tentatively but she was soon caught up in a wave of emotion that made her forget all else. She did not flinch when his hand slipped to her thigh and pulled her flat against his body.

Lois was not totally innocent. She knew what the bulge pressing against her represented. Lying above him, she looked down into his eyes and knew she could bear anything to make him happy.

Lois eased herself away. 'Will you come upstairs with me? You need to be sure. I don't want you to feel trapped if I cannot be a proper wife.'

It took Noah a moment to absorb what she was saying. Her trust was humbling. The words 'trapped' and 'proper wife' had been flung at her, branding her as a failure. He would give his life and soul to erase them.

They did not speak again until, hand in hand, they reached Lois's bedroom. Noah prayed this was not the place where she had been violated. It was a very feminine room decorated in pink and gold. And with an ambience of calm that did not suggest unhappy memories. God willing, what they were about to do would not spoil it. Noah kissed her again, sliding his hand around her back to reach the row of small buttons. One by one he slipped them free until the bodice slid from her shoulders. Her eyes widened when he moved to cup her breast and he stilled. 'I won't do anything you dislike. I will stop if you say so.'

Lois liked the way he was holding her and pressed closer into his hand. He did not squeeze, just lifted her breast higher. His thumb nudged the neck of her dress lower and stroked her soft skin. Lois sighed and her knees threatened to give way. She clung to his shoulders as he lifted her onto the bed. He lay beside her, taking his weight on one elbow so he did not crush her. His lips brushed lightly over her cheek, into the fold of her neck and gradually downwards to the swell of her breast.

Lois felt as though she was floating and did not notice the absence of her bodice until Noah closed his lips over one nipple. Her hips jerked and a sudden rush of wetness made her sit up in alarm.

Noah immediately drew back. 'You want me to stop?' It was almost a groan.

Lois was blushing and would not look at him. 'I am so sorry. You are going to be disgusted. I must get up.' Noah caught her wrist as she slid to the far side of the bed. 'Disgusted?' he repeated.

Lois's face reddened further. Her voice was almost too low for him to catch her words. 'I have wet the bed.' He almost laughed. She was so innocent. 'Lois, look at me.'

She turned her head slowly, afraid of what she might see. 'My darling girl, you liked what I was doing. Your body liked it and wanted more. What you felt was a welcome I hardly dared hope for.'

He allowed her to stand and slid to the edge of the bed without letting go of her wrist. He gently turned her so she was standing between his knees. It took a few minutes for him to explain the details Sarah had not mentioned in her pre-wedding talk and a few more to urge her out of the rest of her clothes. The restraint was almost killing him as the last of her garments slid to the floor.

'You are so perfect,' he murmured like a pray.

Lois looked at him shyly. 'Don't you want to take your things off?'

His voice nearly failed him. 'If you will help me.'

Lois gradually forgot her own nakedness as Noah continued to stroke her while she concentrated on undoing his waistcoat and shirt buttons. She pulled the shirt over his head and gazed at the sprinkling of hair across his chest. Her courage almost failed when it came to the fastening of his trousers. 'I can do that if you will untie my shoelaces,' Noah murmured. He held the flap closed until Lois was upright and turned to one side as he kicked off his shoes and let his trousers fall. He felt fit to burst and feared she might run from the room when she saw his erection. He did not take the risk. In one movement he turned, pulled Lois against his chest and fell backwards onto the bed.

Lois was actually laughing as she looked down into his face. 'Are you shy too?' She wriggled so she could look down, and her eyes widened. 'Does that hurt?'

'A little but it will be better soon.' He did not allow her any more questions and rolled her sideways. Kisses and caresses that she had never dreamed were possible soon had her panting. She was out of her mind, wanting something she did not understand.

Noah eased himself between her legs, careful not to weigh her down. He paused. 'Lois, are you sure? I can still stop.' He was going to die if she said yes, but he had promised.

Lois nodded. He moved as slowly as he could, entering a little and waiting for her to adjust.

She had just got used to the feel of him inside her when he started to draw back and her natural instincts took over. Her arms came around his waist, her legs around his thighs, and her hips rose to meet him.

It was over in a few seconds. Noah sagged to one side, taking Lois with him, and lay with his face buried in the curve of her shoulder.

Lois lay very still, waiting for his verdict. He had not rushed to get away, which seemed like a good sign. He was so still she thought he might even have fallen asleep, so she did not think she had done anything to offend him. She could feel the steady beat of his heart and his breath against her skin. She widened her awareness to absorb the feel of his weight across her arm and one of his legs still between her thighs. She wanted to stay like this forever but the arm beneath him was becoming numb and she moved her fingers.

Noah opened his eyes to see Lois watching him. She looked pale and slightly apprehensive. It was not the look he had hoped for. And it was his own fault. He had tried to be gentle so as not to alarm and send her into a trance, receptive but not engaged. Her responses had been pure instinct, which was promising. He had the rest of his life to teach her about passion. The thought stirred him and he fought down the urge to love her again.

'Are you alright?' he asked.

'I need to move my arm.'

Noah shifted to release it and gathered Lois against his chest. Now her face was hidden so he could not see her expression as he repeated his question.

Lois nodded. 'Thank you. That was rather lovely.'

Faint praise, Noah thought in frustration. 'I should be thanking you.' The words were out before he realised they sounded grudging, a polite response to a compliment.

Lois moved to look at him. There was a slight frown across his brow and his lips had tightened. 'Do you want to withdraw your proposal?'

Noah sat up with a jerk. 'No! Do you want me to?'

'No, but I want you to be happy.'

Noah shook his head in wonderment. Her courage and willingness to put his needs above her own were beyond words. He bent his head to kiss her and she felt his erection pressing against her side. 'Do you want to do it again?' she asked shyly.

It was all the encouragement Noah needed. She was with him all the way and their second loving left them both flushed and out of breath. 'Oh, my,' Lois breathed. Two words that made Noah want to shout for joy.

The rested for a while until Lois asked, 'Will we be married in Australia? There is not enough time to arrange it before you leave.'

'I am not going anywhere. You are going to have the biggest, best wedding Stapleton has ever seen. I want the world to know you are mine.'

Lois took that to mean he would delay his departure. She wondered briefly what would happen to Laington, but it no longer seemed very important. All she wanted was to be with Noah and, hopefully, make love many more times.

Noah stayed with her until the sky started to lighten with a new day. He reluctantly eased himself from the bed and quietly gathered up his scattered clothing, which he took through to what he thought was her dressing room. It was in fact her parlour but it would do. He closed the connecting door and as he turned, came face to face with George's portrait.

The face was so like Gramp, Noah felt like a boy again, caught out in some mischief. 'I am going to marry her,' he muttered before he laughed. He was apologising to a painting! Noah turned his back and pulled on his clothes before looking at the portrait more closely. There were differences but too few to doubt George and Ernest had been related. He wondered if Lois knew they were not blood-brothers.

And did it matter? He would not tell her and diminish the memory of the old man whom she had adored.

Noah was grateful the servants used the hidden stairs so there was no chance of him bumping into them on his way back to his own room. He had not taken into account the fact that Fred was also used to rising early and that the newlyweds had been given one of the best rooms in the west wing. The two men came face to face with a start of surprise. Fred took in Noah's dishevelled appearance and the door he had just closed. He grinned, punched Noah lightly on the arm, and whispered, 'Congratulations.'

Chapter 25

Lois woke slowly and, without opening her eyes, reached out to touch Noah. He was gone. In just a second her disappointment changed to amusement. Of course he was gone. He would not have wanted Sarah to catch him in her bed. Years ago, when Lois's body was changing from child to woman, Sarah had told her what it meant and stressed that certain activities must not be indulged in before marriage, whatever a man told her. Lois could just imagine her boxing Noah's ears!

She was still chuckling to herself when Sarah brought in her early morning tea.

'Do you want me to bring up your breakfast?' Sarah asked.

Lois sat up. 'Whatever for?'

Sarah jerked her head towards Lois's clothes on the floor and the untucked bedding. 'It looks as though you had a disturbed night.'

Lois blushed. 'We are going to be married.'

'The sooner the better if you ask me.' Sarah was trying to sound stern but Lois could hear warm approval in her tone. 'Now drink that tea or your washing water will be cold as well.'

Noah loitered at the top of the stairs, waiting for Lois to leave her room. He greeted her with a light kiss on her cheek and offered his arm so they could descend the stairs together.

'I would like you to be the first to hear that we are going to be married,' Noah told Pound when they reached the hall. Lois was surprised the butler took the sudden he news so calmly. He offered congratulations and told them Mr and Mrs Norton were breakfasting in their room. Lois thought she must be imagining things when Pound turned his head slightly and winked at Noah.

Beneath her hand, Lois could feel Noah chuckling as he led her into the breakfast room. 'What is going on?' she asked suspiciously.

Noah saw her settled at the table and, taking her hand, explained.

'Did you wonder where I went yesterday morning?' Lois nodded. 'I was arranging our future. I was not sure you would agree to marry me before the sailing date and went to warn the others that they would be travelling without me. I also told Pound to delay the removal of Gramp's portrait. There was no point in causing damage if it could be avoided.'

'What would you have done if I had refused?'

'I would have stayed on and asked you again every day until you agreed. I cannot live without you.' He leant forward and kissed her. 'You cannot imagine my relief when you said you wanted me more than Laington.'

Lois frowned in thought. 'What are you going to do with the estate? It is not fair for us to just go off and leave everything adrift.'

It was Noah's turn to frown. 'Lois, we are not going anywhere. I am sure I told you I was going to stay. Love is all, remember. Home is with your loved one.'

'You want to stay? But what about your daughter? I thought you wanted to go home to her.'

'I am ashamed to say I have very little feeling for her. When Clara died, I had a duty to ensure the survival of her child and took her to Clara's sister. I only saw her once more. Diana, Clara's sister, begged me not to take her away as she loved her like her own child. I allowed myself to be persuaded, reasoning that she was too young to travel. I agreed to a temporary arrangement and would see how things were when I returned.' Noah paused to gauge Lois's reaction.

'You were so adamant that you wanted to return to Australia.' Lois looked and sounded worried. 'I don't want you to be unhappy.'

'My happiness is with you.' He leant across to kiss her again and came to a decision. 'Lois, will you walk with me outside? I have things to say that need to be looked at from a different angle.'

It was an intriguing statement and Lois's curiosity was aroused. Noah kept hold of her hand until they had left the house and walked some distance away. He turned her to face the building.

'We both believe love is all that matters but we have been influenced by other people's views. Tell me what you see.'

Lois looked at the house that had been her home for almost as long as she could remember, but she did not think Noah was asking for a description. 'I don't know what you mean.'

'I knew nothing about Laington beyond Gramp's revelations after I received George's letter. He was old and tired. The letter reminded him of a past he had tried to forget.' Noah led Lois to a bench and sat with his arm around her. She listened, comparing his assumptions to the reality he had discovered.

For the first eleven years of his life, Ernest had travelled around Europe with his theatrical family. His father had been a successful actor and playwright, his mother an actress. His aunt Ashley, whom he had only known as Gloria Morrow, was a renowned singer. They were all wilful and could be temperamental. Feelings were expressed. There were arguments and forgiveness. The company they kept had no fixed routine or abode.

Everything had changed when his father's two elder brothers died and Arthur became direct heir to the barony. He was recently widowed and he decided to return to England so his sons could receive a proper education.

Ernest had hated England. He found the buttoned-up attitude of English society stifling and rather dishonest. He had rebelled, refusing to settle at school or take any interest in his future inheritance.

He had also disliked his grandfather, the eleventh baron whom he saw as proud, cold and rigid in his ideas. It had cumulated in his affair with Jenna, a married woman, and his grandfather had banished him until the affair had blown over. It was never meant to be permanent but the affair did not die out. He had kept in touch until his father died and the baron ordered him to come home, without his mistress. That was the final straw.

'Gramp wrote to say that, when the time came, he would sell the estate and build a theatre. Then he made sure he could not be located.'

Noah turned Lois to face him. 'I came here full of contempt for an ancestry that put possessions above love. I meant to sell the estate and fulfil Gramp's ambition.' Noah smiled. 'Then I found you.'

Lois had to wait until he finished kissing her before he continued. 'I loved Gramp but I am not like him. When we acquired the sheep farm, I enjoyed having a settled base. Caring for the stock, seeing the seasons change and things grow gave a purpose that had been missing from my life. But I don't feel compelled to devote my life to it. I want to make my home here, with you.'

'Now I know what you meant about being influenced by other people,' Lois said quietly. 'I loved George. I wanted to please him, which meant loving Laington.' She snuggled closer into Noah's arms and rested her head on his shoulder. 'George never considered Laington to be his. He loved everything about it and loved caring for it but said he was just keeping it safe until Ernest or a descendent was found. He delayed accepting the barony for nearly ten years, until Ernest was officially declared dead. But he never gave up hoping.' Lois paused before adding, quietly, 'George was not Arthur's son.'

'I know. Have you ever studied the family picture?'

Lois smiled. 'George is sitting on his mother's lap in a picture painted by his father. Arthur had told George the truth when he was old enough to understand, but George never ceased to think of Ernest as his brother.'

Noah huffed out a rueful laugh. 'I did not know whether I ought to mention that. Whether it would distress you.'

'Why? A child does not choose its parents. If there is any blame it lies with them.'

Noah tightened his arm. 'Marry me soon. I want our children born on the right side of the blankets.'

Lois blushed and turned back to practical matters. 'What about Ernest's dream? How will you build his theatre if we keep Laington?'

Noah chuckled. 'I am not sure he really meant it. It was probably just a threat to annoy his grandfather. The only time he mentioned it was when he was telling me about his refusal to return to England.'

They lapsed into a contented silence and allowed their thoughts to drift.

Lois was fitting Noah's recent information into what she knew about Ernest. George's recollections of his brother were blurred by time and distance. He had loved and admired a daring, rebellious boy and had no real knowledge of the man Ernest had become. By contrast, George was modest and rather shy. He had come under the influence of his grandfather while he was still an infant and grown up absorbing the ethics of duty and pride in one's heritage. His father spent little time at Laington until the eleventh baron grew infirm, but he had no deep interest in the estate. As soon as George reached age of twenty-one, Arthur gladly handed over the reins and returned to his preferred way of life.

George had brought Lois up along the same lines.

Noah's thoughts were similar but centred on a different pair of brothers.

Bill and Fred had been born into a poor, working-class family with strong moral values. Duty to family was based on love, not possessions. When their lives had been torn apart, they still had that firm base and spent years trying to find each other. Education had turned Fred into a confident, competent man while Bill had been forced to hide his true character beneath a cloak of meekness.

Noah liked Lois's idea of turning Laington into a school for the under-privileged. But he also wanted a home for the family he hoped to have with Lois. He was considering how the house might be divided when Lois spoke.

'I did not like Mr Harris. Will you mind if we transfer our business to another lawyer?'

The out-of-the-blue comment took Noah by surprise and Lois laughed. 'I need to resign my stewardship.'

Noah hugged her. He had forgotten that she was still in control. 'I still have a lot to learn. We will manage Laington together, partners as well as lovers.'

Lois looked at him coyly. 'I like that idea. Will you come to my room again tonight?'

Noah would have liked to carry her upstairs right away. He kissed her and asked, 'How long does it take to arrange a wedding?' He hoped it would not be too long. They could be discreet but there were risks that did not seem to have occurred to Lois. 'I don't want to damage your reputation.' Her slight frown forced him to point out the risk of pregnancy.

Lois blushed. She knew the facts, but her friends had all been married for longer than nine months before they had a child and her elevated position had sheltered her from gossip about rushed marriages in the wider community.

In an effort to such thoughts at bay, Lois returned to her previous subject. 'There is a very good lawyer in Stapleton. George foresaw problems if Laington passed to someone who found a way to disregard his wishes. I would not have been homeless as I have assets but he thought it wise to distance them from the estate. It won't matter once we are married.'

Noah assumed those assets had come through her marriage to Simon Laing. He wanted no part of that! He touched the ring on her left hand. 'Please will you remove that before tonight?'

'It is not my wedding ring,' she assured him. 'It was my mother's. I sold Simon's ring years ago and gave the money to the charity committee.'

Clouds were moving across the sky, and a stiff breeze carried the first spots of rain. Noah took off his jacket and wrapped it around Lois's shoulders. With a quick kiss, he took her hand and they ran back indoors.

They were still hand-clasped and laughing when they burst into the drawing room.

The Nortons stood in a group by the windows, deep in conversation. They stopped talking and turned to face the door. One look at the happy couple told Hattie that all was well and she rushed forward to hug them. The others came more slowly to offer their congratulations and ask questions. Noah suggested they all sit down.

'We will be married as soon as possible.'

'Can that be arranged before we leave?' Fred asked.

Before he had finished speaking, Hattie declared, 'I am not going to miss Lois's wedding.'

'The journey is booked.'

'Noah has made all the arrangements.'

'I don't care.'

Noah held up his hand to stop the babble of voices. 'Stop! Listen to me.' He waited until they were all seated. 'I was going to suggest you delay your departure. I don't know when there will be another ship, but it does not matter. We want you all to be at our wedding.'

Bill was happy to agree but Fred asked, 'What are we to do? I have savings but I need employment as soon as possible. I don't want to lose the job you offered.'

Noah pointed out that no one was expecting them on a certain date.

'We can't impose on you for so long.'

Ruby touched her husband's arm. 'We did not have a wedding trip.' She smiled encouragingly. 'Or I am sure Father would give you temporary employment.'

'I can go back to working for you,' Bill told Lois, adding, 'If you don't mind.'

It took Noah and Lois some time to overcome the Nortons' ingrained work ethic. 'We can find plenty for you to do,' Noah assured them. 'I want our wedding to be the grandest Stapleton has ever seen.' He smiled at Lois. 'You deserve it and the local people need reassuring that I am really here to stay.'

Chapter 26

The news that Noah was to marry Lois and remain at Laington spread quickly through the community. The invisible barrier that had made him feel an outcast was swept away and he was greeted with smiles and congratulations. A notice in the newspapers brought an avalanche of letters from far and wide, too many for them to answer personally, and Hemmings was kept busy drafting replies for them to sign.

The post also brought an aggrieved letter from Mr Harris. After congratulating Noah on taking his advice, he expressed sorrow and dismay that, after years of faithful service, the Laington account was being taken out of his hands. It was couched in polite, long-winded sentences, but Noah could almost hear the man grinding his teeth.

Mr Burrows, the local solicitor, was a man of very different character. He only gave advice when it was asked for and did not question the wisdom of the plans Noah and Lois put before him. He was asked to contact the organisation that had educated Fred Norton. Their experience and help would be of great assistance when they set up their own school. For the time being it was to be kept secret.

Mr Burrows could not see any problem with Noah inheriting the barony, although it would take time to get the necessary verification documents from Australia.

The title was not high on Noah's agenda and he kept to himself the fact that Ernest and Jenna had never married. His main focus was getting his own marriage arranged so that he did not have to creep through the house to join Lois each night.

Lois floated through the waiting period on a cloud of happiness. Her days were filled with arrangements but always, at the back of her mind, was a longing for nightfall and another lesson on loving.

They had decided to alter the bedrooms, and workmen were drafted in to redecorate the late baroness's suite. Its western aspect benefitted from the afternoon and evening sun and one of the rooms would become their private sitting room.

As Lois had the wedding arrangements in hand, Noah spent much of his time touring the house, making notes on how the school could be self-contained without causing too much damage to the structure. Fortunately, the north wing had only been used to store generations of unwanted furniture and artifacts as the fashions changed. They would need to be sorted and either stored elsewhere or sold to make room for dormitories and classrooms. Their monetary value still did not mean a lot to Noah, but he was coming to appreciate quality and craftsmanship.

On a sunny morning in early June, Lois was being dressed for her wedding by the three women closest to her. Sarah stood on a stool behind Lois to lift the gown high over Lois's head while Hattie stood in front to guide Lois's arms into the sleeves without disarranging her hair. The gown was of a dusky pink, ribbed silk, cut in the latest fashion. Lois had refused to have the bodice heavily boned and relied on her own good posture and draped material to give the desired silhouette.

Mary had come to Laington well in advance of the wedding day and used her expert knowledge to guide Lois's choice of design. She had watched over every stage of the gown's construction by a local dressmaker when Lois refused to go to one of the top modistes in London.

Lois was only allowed to look in the mirror when her friends were satisfied with her appearance. As a widow, Lois could not wear a veil so a tiara of pearls and rubies surrounded her upswept and curled hair. A matching necklace and bracelet completed the ensemble. The result was much more elaborate than anything Lois would have chosen alone, but Noah had wanted grandeur.

Lois turned this way and that, thinking she looked like one of the princesses in the story books Sarah used to read to her as a child. 'Thank you,' she said to the friends reflected in the mirror. The words were inadequate to express how she felt but more would have brought her to tears.

Sarah moved to answer a knock at the door. Ruby, who had spent much of the past month with her family in Bristol, poked her head inside and asked if they could come in. Receiving a nod, she and Mrs Drayton entered the room.

Mrs Drayton clasped her hands to her bosom, closer to tears than Lois had been. 'Oh, my dear girl! Noah is going to be so stunned. You look beautiful.'

Ruby added her own good wishes, remembering that Lois's previous marriage had been a very dowdy affair in midwinter and followed by tragedy. She had too much tact to speak her thoughts aloud.

It was inevitable that similar thoughts had occurred to Lois. She pushed them aside. The past was gone, unlamented. She was no longer a naïve girl, bowing to other people's wishes. Noah's love had given her the confidence to acknowledge her own worth. She had a right to happiness and grasped it with both hands.

Stapleton turned out in force to witness the marriage of the thirteenth baron to the lady who had held the estate together for several years.

Noah was employer, landlord and benefactor. His position demanded deference but he was earning true respect on his own behalf with some of the projects he had already started. News of the proposed school would be announced at the reception.

Lois was known, admired and loved. They honoured her for taking on the responsibility without the airs and graces of the previous baroness. What they thought of her previous husband was muttered in private as people recalled instances of his arrogance and cruelty to animals. His death had been unlamented and they were glad Lois was to be baroness, as she deserved.

The shops and houses around the marketplace were decorated with flags and streamers. Stalls, run by the local tavern keepers, had been set up so everyone present could drink the health of the bride and groom when they emerged from the church after the ceremony. The bakers were to provide penny buns for the children.

Killjoys like Mrs Grainger criticised Noah's generosity and predicted a wave of drunkenness and disorder, but Noah trusted the taverners. They would not begin serving until the bells heralded the end of the service and knew their customers. There would be little time for the eager to gain extra refills. On top of that, the wave of goodwill was such that Noah did not believe anyone would behave badly and spoil the day.

There were cheers when he arrived at the church and he took a moment to call out a general thank you. If that was how they greeted him, Noah suspected Lois's arrival would be heard miles away.

The inside of the church was festooned with flowers, and children lined the aisle with baskets of petals to strew in Lois's path. The air had a buzz of expectation. The invited guests sat close to the front, talking quietly but, further back, the less inhibited called greetings to Noah as he and Bill made their way to the altar.

Bill had demurred at being chosen as best man until Noah told him he did not know of a better man. He meant it, unaware that it also raised his standing with the general population. The mayor had tentatively offered to support Noah, whose refusal was softened by asking the man to propose the toast from the church steps.

Cheers from outside almost drowned out the sound of the bells. The organist changed from gentle background music to a triumphant march. Everyone rose to their feet and Noah turned to look down the aisle. He could not see Lois at first as the main door was to one side and the congregation blocked his view.

As Lois, with her hand resting on Rev Dunn's arm, stepped onto the central aisle, Noah caught his breath. She was small but her radiance filled the church, and his heart swelled with pride. The children started to throw their petals in her path and Lois smiled at each one as she passed.

Noah did not remember much of the actual service. As soon as Rev Dunn placed Lois's hand in his, all else faded. She gazed up at him with a soft, tender smile and squeezed his fingers. They made their responses without taking their eyes off each other. When the vicar pronounced them man and wife, there was a collective sigh from the congregation. Noah did not wait to be told he could kiss the bride and lowered his head. The kiss was firm but not devouring. It was homage and more meaningful than the words he had just spoken. She was his to have and hold, love and cherish through all that life could throw at them. Together they were complete, two halves of a wonderful whole. Noah was not much of one for praying but he was thanking God that he had found her.

Lois was overwhelmed by the look on Noah's face. She thought she knew him well but something magical had just happened. He had told her he loved her on many occasions, demonstrated it in many ways, but never before had she felt so loved and cherished.

The vicar had to ask twice before he had their attention. 'Signing the register,' he reminded them quietly and led the way to the vestry.

When they emerged, a large number of the congregation had left their seats, leaving whose who meant most to Noah and Lois to follow them down the aisle.

The joyful pealing of the bells and loud cheers greeted their arrival on the front steps.

The mayor raised his hand for silence and made a short speech. He waited until most, if not all, had obtained a drink before calling, 'To Baron and Lady Laing. Long life and happiness!'

'And lots of children!' Mrs Whittaker's voice carried above the tumult, causing laughter to join the cheers.

The photographer Noah had engaged began shooing everyone but the bridal couple off the steps and disappeared under the black cloth of his camera. There was no need of his instruction to smile. Keeping it in place for the required time was hard.

'My jaw is going to set solid,' Noah muttered, and Lois burst out laughing. The photographer ducked out of his hiding place and said he would have to do it again.

Noah promised as many pictures as the man wanted once they were back at the manor. Their decorated carriage had arrived and everyone was eager to see them on their way with the rattle of pots and pans and a shower of thrown flowers.

'My lady,' Noah whispered as he helped Lois into the open carriage.

'My husband,' Lois whispered in return, earning a kiss that raised cheers from the crowd.

Tenant epilogue

Ten years later.

Mrs Whittaker had her wish and lived to see the first of Noah and Lois's four children christened.

She also witnessed the crocodile of uniformed children who filed into church each Sunday.

The proposed school had met with varied reactions from the local community. Some dreaded the influx of down and outs, predicting a wave of crime and hooliganism. Others welcomed the chance of extra employment and applauded the baron and baroness for extending their benefaction to the less fortunate.

The school had not materialised overnight. There was advice to be sought and building work to be done. The organisers of the London Society that had educated Fred were more than happy to help. Noah and Lois visited the school and the organisers visited Laington. Together they formulated a plan that suited (nearly) everyone.

The pupils were selected with the help of local charities. There was no shortage of orphans or needy children in Stapleton and the surrounding towns. In collaboration with Mr Collins and the Stapleton school governors, the younger children were taught in the refurbished town school and the older pupils at the manor. A similar system dealt with the children's accommodation. The young ones were fostered into families and the senior members at the manor. It was an unusual and forward-thinking arrangement that drew attention from far and wide, most of it positive. Gradually, Noah was drawn into campaigning for better education for all.

Some of the manor's formal rooms were kept for the baron and baroness's public duties. Others were turned into enlarged offices to deal with the different aspects of their lives.

Noah and Lois were true partners. Lois continued to oversee the house and work with the local community. Noah concentrated on the land, industrial and financial aspects of their holdings, but their duties were not exclusive. Major issues were discussed and agreed jointly.

The same applied to their private lives.

They had their own private rooms, separate from the school and offices, where they created a cosy home and lived without undue ceremony. A small staff enabled them to carry out their duties and still have time to spend with their growing family.

Neither had any experience of a settled family unit, but love and common sense filled the gaps. Adam was born to novice parents still in the throes of a passionate love affair. Noah had been anxious every day of Lois's first pregnancy, but she sailed through the experience in the same calm and practical way she dealt with any situation. She coped with the early symptoms by adjusting her timetable but bloomed in the latter months and a trouble-free confinement.

She was wise enough to recruit experienced help in caring for her child but both she and Noah were very involved in his nurture.

Bethany joined the well-established nursery fourteen months later. There was a gap of four years before Daniel arrived, quickly followed by Tamsin.

Noah and Lois were still very much in love but it had matured to a solid foundation upon which everything else depended. Their children thrived in an atmosphere of love, security and respect.

Life was good and as they approached their tenth wedding anniversary, they hoped the celebrations would include the advent of another child.

But that is another story.